Mafia King

Also From Rachel Van Dyken

Mafia Royals
Royal Bully
Ruthless Princess
Scandalous Prince
Destructive King
Fallen Royal, coming soon

Liars, Inc.
Dirty Exes
Dangerous Exes

Covet Series
Stealing Her
Finding Him

Bro Code Series
Co-Ed
Seducing Mrs. Robinson
Avoiding Temptation
The Set-Up

Elite Bratva Brotherhood
Debase

The Players Game Series
Fraternize
Infraction
MVP

The Consequence Series
The Consequence of Loving Colton
The Consequence of Revenge
The Consequence of Seduction
The Consequence of Rejection

Fall
Eternal
Strung
Capture

The Renwick House Series
The Ugly Duckling Debutante
The Seduction of Sebastian St. James
An Unlikely Alliance
The Redemption of Lord Rawlings
The Devil Duke Takes a Bride

The London Fairy Tales Series
Upon a Midnight Dream
Whispered Music
The Wolf's Pursuit
When Ash Falls

The Seasons of Paleo Series
Savage Winter
Feral Spring

The Wallflower Series (with Leah Sanders)
Waltzing with the Wallflower
Beguiling Bridget
Taming Wilde

The Dark Ones Saga
The Dark Ones
Untouchable Darkness
Dark Surrender
Darkest Temptation
Darkest Sinner

Stand-Alones
Mafia Casanova (with M Robinson)
Hurt: A Collection (with Kristin Vayden and Elyse Faber)
Rip
Compromising Kessen

Mafia King

A Mafia Royals Novella

By Rachel Van Dyken

1001 DARK NIGHTS

PRESS

Mafia King: A Mafia Kings Novella
By Rachel Van Dyken
Copyright 2021
ISBN: 978-1-951812-27-0

Published by 1001 Dark Nights Press, an imprint of Evil Eye Concepts, Incorporated

Sign up for the 1001 Dark Nights Newsletter
and be entered to win a Tiffany Key necklace.

There's a contest every month!

Go to www.1001DarkNights.com to subscribe.

As a bonus, all subscribers can download
FIVE FREE exclusive books!

Acknowledgments from the Author

I'm always so thankful to work with the team at 1001 Dark Nights! They are always so awe inspiring! To all the new readers, I hope you enjoy this story and it helps you dive into the mafia head first! To my old readers—this is the one you've been waiting for! Thank you so much for your support! Jill, thank you for not killing me during this deadline and for being the sole beta reader before I turned it in—no pressure! To my incredible team thank you for hanging in there these last few months with new baby, you've been so patient and supportive! Cheers and happy reading!

One Thousand and One Dark Nights

Once upon a time, in the future…

*I was a student fascinated with stories and learning.
I studied philosophy, poetry, history, the occult, and
the art and science of love and magic. I had a vast
library at my father's home and collected thousands
of volumes of fantastic tales.*

*I learned all about ancient races and bygone
times. About myths and legends and dreams of all
people through the millennium. And the more I read
the stronger my imagination grew until I discovered
that I was able to travel into the stories... to actually
become part of them.*

*I wish I could say that I listened to my teacher
and respected my gift, as I ought to have. If I had, I
would not be telling you this tale now.
But I was foolhardy and confused, showing off
with bravery.*

*One afternoon, curious about the myth of the
Arabian Nights, I traveled back to ancient Persia to
see for myself if it was true that every day Shahryar
(Persian: شهریار, "king") married a new virgin, and then
sent yesterday's wife to be beheaded. It was written
and I had read, that by the time he met Scheherazade,
the vizier's daughter, he'd killed one thousand
women.*

Something went wrong with my efforts. I arrived in the midst of the story and somehow exchanged places with Scheherazade – a phenomena that had never occurred before and that still to this day, I cannot explain.

Now I am trapped in that ancient past. I have taken on Scheherazade's life and the only way I can protect myself and stay alive is to do what she did to protect herself and stay alive.

Every night the King calls for me and listens as I spin tales. And when the evening ends and dawn breaks, I stop at a point that leaves him breathless and yearning for more. And so the King spares my life for one more day, so that he might hear the rest of my dark tale.

As soon as I finish a story... I begin a new one... like the one that you, dear reader, have before you now.

Prologue

Tank

"I'm in Hell." I hung my head in my hands, not giving a shit if Sergio Abandonato, made man, doctor for the Five Families, and truly genuine pain in my FBI ass pulled a gun on me.

Hell, at this point, I'd welcome a knife.

If he told me he was going to cut off my dick and feed it to his chickens—crazy I know, can't talk about it, too traumatized, carry on—I'd be like...do it, put me out of my fucking misery.

Now.

I beg you!

It all started a year ago. The FBI decided that they wanted me to infiltrate Chicago's most notorious mafia Families by way of their kids—most of which were my age and attending Eagle Elite University. It sounded like an easy in-and-out job—and then I got to know them. Really know them. And realized that not only was I semi-related by way of my dead parents, but they were also more loyal than any agent I'd ever worked with. I never expected to start working for all five of the most powerful bosses in the Cosa Nostra—to kill for them...look the other way. Or to justify everything they did all in the name of blood and loyalty. But I did.

And now Sergio was looking at me like I had no choice but to do his bidding—again. And smiled while doing it.

I'd never been weak. Never.

Until I met his eldest daughter.

Kartini Abandonato. Or, to most of the Family: Tiny.

Cute, right?

If you're a huge fan of blood-sucking piranhas, then sure, super-cute. But me? I'm more of a dog guy. So, no, she wasn't cute.

Oh, she was beautiful.

But cute?

Friendly?

House-trained?

That would be a no.

Even now, I could picture her walking into the kitchen wearing a skin-tight leather leotard with a plunging neckline, heels that could kill a man dead, heavy eye makeup, with one hand full of a bottle of Jack, and the other holding her ever-present vape pen.

Tame?

My. Ass.

And that was the thing. She used to be this...tiny, adorable thing.

Now, she was my job.

My purpose.

Basically, despite our seven-year age difference...she was my job. The girl I guarded, watched over, made sure to keep alive—and all because I'd refused them.

Who?

The Five Families.

They wanted my loyalty.

And I told them I wanted to toe the line between the FBI and the Five Families in order to help.

HELP.

They said they didn't want help.

But they needed it.

So, I fell on my sword.

And now?

Punished.

"You'll do it," her father said with a grin, his hair pulled into a sleek man bun as he sipped his glass of red wine or whatever the hell it was. His smile was amused, all white and cheerful like he had something to be happy about despite the devil owning his daughter's soul. "And you'll do it well. Otherwise..." He trained his revolver on me and shrugged. "Target practice."

"You have chickens for that," I deadpanned.

He laughed. "No, I have you for that."

"How...comforting." I shifted in my seat. "Look, I get that she needs protection, what with her sudden desire to push every rebel button in the history of rebellion, but I'm still working for the FBI.

Asking me to be her personal guard and keep the Families out of the shit is crap, and you know it!"

"First off..." He stood. "We already told you to cut the shit and tell the FBI no. They'll understand, they're used to our..."—he shrugged— "methods." He sighed. "And, second, she needs someone outside the immediate family. Someone who isn't a dad or a cousin or an uncle who's breathing down her neck."

I hated that he had a point. Every time he trained an associate on her, she pushed a little bit harder.

And I lost a bit more of my free time.

I squeezed my eyes shut. "How long?"

"Two more weeks."

I perked right up. "That's it?" And then my death sentence was done?

His grin was cruel. "That's it."

I nodded. "Well, two weeks is...it's almost a kindness. Thank you. I'll just be seeing myself out now and—"

"In Mexico."

I froze, a chill ran down my spine. "Mexico?" Where everything was legal?

"Family vacation. Aka Junior and Serena are eloping," he added as a massive hand came down on my shoulder. "You're Family. We need a vacation, her cousins are eloping, she needs to be reined in, so...of course, you'll come and help out."

I'd never been more tempted to run in the opposite direction of another human, and I'd trained at Quantico. "For two weeks." I just had to repeat it.

"Tomorrow, ten a.m. The jet won't wait for you, and if you miss it, neither will my bullet...clear?"

I gulped, clenching my fists a dozen times before nodding my head once and gritting out, "As glass."

"Great! See you in the morning!" A cheerful shove toward the door, and then I was walking out of his house.

The house I'd been living in for months—nearly a year.

The house that offered a double agent protection.

The house that the devil, too, resided in.

And just in time, her jet-black Lambo roared into the circular driveway.

Oh, good.

Let's just hope she was clothed and sober.

She really was the worst.

The car jerked to a stop, turned off, and then there she was, every small, curvy inch of her as she hopped out on her red stiletto heels and turned toward me, a smile building on her lips as she tugged off her black sunglasses and sauntered toward me smelling like seduction and addiction.

Yay.

Her red lips parted.

I needed to look away.

There was too much temptation and sin in that small part.

And I knew if I even once gave in to the thoughts in my head…

She'd eat me alive.

And I'd fucking let her.

God, I hated her.

For her power.

Her control.

For being the smartest woman in the room and knowing it.

Really, the list was long, exhaustive, and depressing to a spy like me.

"You still alive?" she asked.

I glared. "You still a virgin?"

"Aww, you feeling horny, old man?"

I gritted my teeth. "I'm not old."

"And I'm not a virgin."

I smirked. "I'll just add that to the long list of things to tell your dad after the two weeks are over, then."

"Two weeks? What do you mean, two weeks? You're done. You were done days ago."

My turn to offer a smug grin as I leaned in and whispered in her ear, "We're going on vacation. And I was just blessed with the job of being your shadow. Happy early birthday."

She gasped, stumbling backward. "He wouldn't."

"He would. He did. He's mafia, what did you expect? A normal birthday party with a piñata while your cousins got married on the beach?"

"Okay, first off, that's not normal for a grown-ass woman. Second, he said it was a gift, the vacation. For my birthday. Third, it was only supposed to be my cousins and me, my favorite cousins—you aren't one of them! And I may have completely forgotten about the elopement."

I rolled my eyes. "I'm not your cousin, Tiny!"

Her nostrils flared. "Believe me, I know. At least my cousins know how to shoot, and fight, and—"

I grabbed her by the arm and flipped her back against her car, causing her sunglasses to fall to the ground as her body arched up to meet me. "I'm the fucking government. I'm the one who arrests you for doing things...shall we say, improper? I'm your new judge, jury, and executioner. If you so much as break any laws, mafia or mine, I will report it. I may not be blood, but I know our rules and I serve the Family, not you. NEVER. You. Do you feel me?"

Her breath hitched, and then she bucked her hips against mine and whispered, "Oh...was that it, then? I. Felt. Nothing."

I jerked back, only to have her hand grab at my dick. "Ah, there it is... Pity, for a man so large, you seem so very... Small."

I shoved her hand away and grabbed at her tits. "Same, Tiny. Same."

Her eyes widened in rage, but I was already walking in the other direction despite her cussing and yelling.

Two weeks in hell.

Two weeks with Satan's mistress.

Two weeks left, and my fate with the mafia would be decided.

I just hoped I survived the cursed princess.

And the mean streak she seemed to have developed overnight.

A job.

It was a job.

And I was trained for everything.

So Kartini Abandonato?

Not a problem.

Never.

If anything, I was about to raise hell with her, and there was nothing she could do about it.

I smiled the entire drive to my friend Ash's house.

Time to spar.

Time to imagine blood on my hands.

Time to feel.

Time to let go of the numbness.

And exist.

Outside of whatever fucking Kartini Abandonato had to offer.

Chapter One

Kartini

One Year Ago...

I was dancing on my dad's shoes as if I were still fourteen or younger when, really, I was seventeen going on eighteen. Wow, another year younger, and I'd be in the *Sound of Music.*

Sigh.

My dad was my everything.

Strong.

Brave.

Compassionate.

Oh, yeah, and he was *sort of* like a made man, killer, and doctor to the Five Families of Chicago.

Shrug.

But I never really saw him as this evil person; I couldn't. Not with his gentle smile, his fierce protectiveness, and the way he always looked at me like I was his world.

And every single time, I believed it.

Because my father may kill the bad guys to keep me safe, he may save the assassins by stitching them up, but one thing my father was not was a liar.

"You're getting too old," he grumbled, spinning us again as we danced at my cousin's wedding.

I loved that even in his early fifties, he looked better than Brad Pitt. People always asked me why my dad was so young. *Well, folks, he's not young. He's just an Abandonato, through and through.*

I mean, seriously, what did they put in the water? I giggled as I looked around at all my tatted-up uncles, the bosses, the badasses of the Cosa Nostra.

They were the law.

And it treated them well.

Just like aging.

I sighed as Breaker and Violet came out onto the dance floor. My cousin and her husband were perfect for each other, happy in every way I craved.

As much as I knew what was expected of me in the Family, I also had this small hope that it wouldn't just be about killing for blood, protecting, dying one day—that it would be about an actual family.

Mine.

I wanted kids.

Not one.

Not two.

I literally wanted a plethora of them—something I was sure would send any sane man screaming into the night. But that was the guy you didn't want—the screamer. Nah, I wanted the yeller, the one who announced to everyone and everything how much he loved me, how much he loved his kid despite having a continuous trail of ketchup down his designer shirt.

I wanted the warmth.

The love.

What my parents had raised me in.

And what I'd craved growing up—more siblings, despite all the family I already had.

With a sigh, I pulled back from my dad as he leaned down and kissed my forehead. "Are you okay?"

"Dad…" I shrugged. "Are any of us ever just okay?"

His eyes darted from left to right, and then he rolled them. "You're too smart."

"I'm your kid."

"Yes." His nostrils flared, and his eyes darkened. "You. Are."

"Dad—"

"Don't *Dad* me." He pulled me close again. "Let them all see how much I love my daughter. Let them know how precious you are, how I would move mountains, oceans, skies—you are mine, and one day, you'll look at someone with those gorgeous blue eyes and see the world. One day, it won't be me on the other end of that awestruck look you've always worn on your face. One day, I will walk you down an aisle, I will give you to another man, and I will feel lost. So fucking lost, Tiny. Because how does a protector? A man? A father? Trust something so precious in the hands of someone who's not his own?"

Tears filled my eyes as I smiled up into perfection. The man I would measure everyone against—my daddy. "You can't, Daddy. That's why you have the gun and get to pull the trigger if they fail."

He barked out a laugh. "That's my bloodthirsty girl."

"Up top." I held my hand up for a high-five and earned one from Dad before we both burst into laughter.

"Serg." The Petrov boss, Andrei, approached in all his golden, godlike beauty—damn, he was fine. "A quick word?"

"Yup." Dad leaned down and kissed my forehead again, whispering, "Stay out of trouble."

"Please." I rolled my eyes. "I'm the epitome of perfection."

Dad stared.

And Andrei? He shook his head and murmured, "Girls terrify me."

Dad just laughed. "And yet, you have one."

Andrei looked heavenward. "My point exactly."

His little girl wasn't so little anymore, but she did just turn sixteen. I imagined the fact that she was driving kept him up at night more than all the kills under his belt.

"Stay safe," Dad reminded me, his full lips pressed into a smile. We both knew that out of my younger sister and me, I was as pure as the newly fallen snow—I lived for his approval.

Gladly.

And he knew it.

God, I'd rather die than disappoint him.

"Promise." I waved with my fingertips then made my way over to the cash bar. My brown hair was pulled into a loosely braided bun at the base of my neck, and pieces of hair tickled my skin as I attempted to walk across the grass in ridiculously high electric-blue heels.

One of the first pairs I'd ever purchased with the unlimited credit card that every Abandonato heir was given.

People stared, but they always did. I was Kartini Abandonato, *Tiny* to my cousins because of my short stature—and a daddy's girl through and through.

But it wasn't just that.

It wasn't like I was vain, not even a little bit. And it wasn't even that my mom told me on a daily basis how striking I was.

It was just the knowledge that I'd hit the perfect mixture of both parents' gene pools and came out from the deep end like a freaking mermaid.

From the perfect smattering of freckles across my nose.

To the naturally full lips and high cheekbones. And, of course, the dimples that had every guy—bad and good—falling all over themselves to help me.

My legs wobbled a bit on the grass, and I immediately had two guys rushing over, both who'd been staring for the past few minutes.

"Are you okay?" The golden Adonis held my elbow, his smile wide, his teeth straight and perfect.

"That was a rough fall…" the other said. He had a strong jaw and hair that fell across his forehead in a perfect messy arrangement of jet-black curls.

I smiled my appreciation. "Thanks, boys, but I'm a big girl."

"Yeah, you are," dark hair said, earning a smack from golden hair.

I threw back my head and laughed, then whispered, "You're gonna have to try harder than that if you want my attention. And a little bit of advice, when you get my attention, you also get his." I turned and pointed at my dad, who was at that very moment pulling back his suit jacket to reveal not one but two guns strapped to his chest.

I nearly did fall when they both released me with excuses.

"Yeah, I gotta…go…pee," said dark.

"Alcohol." Golden made a beeline for one of the two open bars, nearly tripping over his feet.

Huh, they were sexy.

Now, they just looked like scared little boys.

I grinned and shook my head, then continued making my way toward the bar near the water.

"It's rude, you know…" a rich, masculine voice said from behind me.

I recognized it instantly.

Recognized *him*.

How could I not?

If there was one man in the entire world that my dad would murder for touching me without even hearing an excuse—it would be Tank. FBI agent, friend of the Families and the government, made man, and all-around conundrum of goodness and virtue.

I bet he sported red power ties and carried a briefcase when he wasn't with us.

I shuddered.

Hot.

Why did Tank in a suit sound so freaking hot?

I glanced over my shoulder. "You're still alive?"

"Haha." He rolled his eyes. "Where's your babysitter?"

"I'm looking at him." I winked.

He paled instantly.

"WOW!" I kept laughing. "At least now I know how you feel about me. Keeping watch over me makes you physically ill, memo received."

"No. Yes…" He ran a hand through his rich chocolate-and-honey-colored hair. It was thick, I-used-to-be-a-quarterback-in-high-school perfection. "It's just…I have enough Abandonatos on my ass right now. The last thing I need is one more using me for target practice."

"Oh, he has a guy for that."

"Pardon?"

I shrugged. "For live target practice. Just has him run back and forth, back and forth, until he tuckers out. I mean, naturally, Dad would never actually hit him, but it does make it more interesting. I think the worst he got was hit in the leg." I examined my pink nails. "Nothing but a flesh wound."

"Says literally no sane person outside of the mafia."

I just repeated what the bosses said on a daily basis. "We're all of us, a bit insane, don't you think?"

"I don't think. I know."

For one brief second, I got lost in his eyes, in the way they drank me in and then shuttered as if he were hiding something.

As if he had something to hide.

Everyone had vetted him.

But it didn't matter, did it?

He looked nervous. And Tank never looked nervous. Furthermore, he wasn't a lingerer, especially with me. Was he trying his hand at being a human shield?

"You headed to the bar?" I started to move as his eyes darted behind me and then around as if he were checking out the perimeter to ensure we were safe when we had hundreds of men on our payroll walking around.

We were safe.

"Yup." He held out his arm. "Now, let me help you walk before you kill yourself or twist an ankle."

"Ah, the perfect gentleman."

He snorted. "You have no idea."

"You're right...I don't. None of us really do outside of when you come and train with the rest of the guys or when you're in class at University. So, what's your dirty secret, huh? You really an old man in his thirties pretending to be twenty-five?"

He stumbled a bit.

"Um, aren't you supposed to be helping me walk, not the other way around?"

"The ground's uneven." He was a shit liar. "And, no, I'm not some creeper in my thirties. Not that thirties is that old. You're just that young, you know? Like when you're in the first grade and suddenly being ten years old is an adult."

"Oh, I've always been one of those."

"A first-grader?"

"An adult." I winked.

His laugh was rich and amused. "Says the girl who's having trouble walking in heels."

"But the ground's uneven..." I licked my lips. "Right?"

His eyes narrowed. "You're terrifying."

"You're like the second old man to tell me that today."

"I'm not an old man!" He raised his voice a bit.

I studied his sculpted biceps and massive body, the way his face had darkened with a hint of five o'clock shadow that always made itself known later in the day and sighed. "Sure, whatever you say."

We stopped in front of the sleek, white marble bar top. "For the lady?"

"Milk," Tank said with a grin.

I smacked him on the arm. Not an inch of fat on him, was there? "I'll have white wine—"

Tank's sigh interrupted me.

"What's your deal, dude?" I elbowed him harder.

"Typical. Perfect daughter. Perfect, innocent little...girl gets boring white wine. I think I'd shit myself if you got anything harder than—"

"Whiskey, neat." I changed my mind and then looked behind him.

"Why the hell are you staring at my ass?" Tank shoved me lightly.

"What?" I laughed. "You said you'd shit yourself. I'm waiting for the storm."

"Disgusting." He sighed, despite the cute bartender hiding a smile.

I grabbed my small glass and lifted it in cheers to Tank. "You're the one who said it."

"See…terrifying," he mumbled. "And as loath as I am to admit it, I'll have what the small child next to me is illegally drinking."

I stuck out my tongue. "I'm not a small child, you asshat. Oh, also, he's on the Abandonato payroll. He checks my ID, he gets checked out"—I paused for drama— "of life."

Tank took his drink and lifted a brow. "That true?"

"I don't ask questions. Whatever the princess wants, the princess gets," he answered wisely and then nodded his head. "Cheers, Miss Abandonato."

"Cheers, cute bartender. Cheers." I lifted my drink in the air and then clinked it with Tank's as we both walked off toward the rest of my cousins. They were all sitting around with numerous bottles of wine, looking as relaxed as I suddenly felt with the whiskey burning down my throat.

Maksim and Izzy were clearly still *on a break.*

Though I had insider information that Chase had threatened to turn Maksim inside out if he kept sneaking into the house, a lot more went down that nobody knew.

Not my story to tell.

And I had to take sides—naturally, I took Izzy's since we were good friends. I couldn't ask for a better cousin.

Then there was Valerian and Violet close by, him in his tux, her in her dress as they slow danced by the group.

Serena, my other cousin, and her boy toy, soon-to-be fiancé, Junior. He had her tucked against him as he played with her hair.

And then there was Ash.

My favorite.

His expression dark, circles under his eyes—I was afraid the most for him.

Not *of* him.

King kept trying to get him involved in the conversation, but it was like every time he said something, it pissed Ash off more, and the alcohol went down his throat like water.

I normally wasn't with those I referred to as the *older cousins*. The Five Families all had a ton of kids, and they kind of arranged us in order from the bigs to the littles. Until you turned eighteen, you weren't allowed to hang out with the bigs because, according to all the dads, they were a bad influence—bloodthirsty, beautiful, scary, loyal, and sometimes, when necessary, mean.

But I was just shy of eighteen now.

I was ready to join.

They'd always tried to include me. I mean, it wasn't like I was a stranger, but I could tell they tried to censor themselves around me. Case in point, the minute Junior saw me, I knew he was going to pull both hands away from Serena's boobs, and she'd stop massaging the obvious bulge in his pants with her one fingertip.

I may not be deadly.

But I noticed everything.

And they were seconds away from sneaking off and screwing against the nearest hard surface.

Tank walked in silence next to me. "Your cousins are all crazy."

"Yup."

"I like it."

"Me, too." I smiled up at him. "It keeps things entertaining."

"You may be small,"—he wrapped an arm around me—"but I'm glad you're finally going to be at the big kids' table, Tiny."

"Awww, Tank, that was very drunkenly heartfelt. Thank you. And might I add I'm very glad you didn't shit yourself earlier? Not a good look if you wanna pick up one of the bridesmaids."

"Righttttttt." He laughed. "Because the one in her sixties was really doing it for me."

"That's a cousin from Italy. Word to the wise, if she makes a beeline for you, cover your dick. She likes to pull things."

"Dicks don't like being pulled."

I put my hand on his shoulder as we got closer. "Exactly."

We shared a smile, and then I heard my name.

What?

My name?

Who was talking about me?

"I'm just saying, I like the group as it is. Now, all the young ones are growing up, and it fucking blowwwwsssss." Serena leaned her head back against Junior's chest. "I mean, we can't even cuss around them!"

"But Kartini isn't so bad." Izzy came to my defense. "I mean, she's gorgeous, knows how to pack a punch, and is super sarcastic."

Ash snorted out a laugh.

"What?" Izzy smacked him on the back of the head.

"I think she'd cry if she saw a dick, lives to please dear old dad like a pathetic little child who needs a pat on the head and a glass of milk before bed, and if I hear her call him 'Daddy' one more time in that syrupy-sweet voice of hers with those fucking dimples, I'm going to lose my shit."

"Ash," Junior warned. "Don't be a dick. Meaning, don't be yourself."

"What?" Ash was clearly drunk. "She doesn't belong here, not with us, not ever. God, can you imagine if she saw half the shit we did? She'd run to Sergio in a heartbeat with crocodile tears in her eyes, and we'd all get the shit beat out of us."

"She wouldn't tell." Izzy glared at her brother. "God, you're even more of an ass than I thought."

"She would." Ash just kept talking. "I'll say it again, Kartini can't hang. She doesn't belong here, and—"

Tank cleared his throat.

I looked down at the shoes I'd had trouble walking in.

And, suddenly, felt like an imposter.

A big, giant fake.

A little girl playing dress-up in her mom's closet, holding her dad's whiskey and pretending she knew the horrors of the world when she'd only ever been shielded from them.

Every single cousin gaped at me, most likely to see if I'd cry or just yell at them. Instead, I handed Tank my drink with a shaking hand, kicked off my stilettos, and threw both of them directly at Ash's drunken face before I turned and ran toward the shore.

Fighting ensued.

Tank's voice rose.

I tried to catch my breath, but it was like there was no air for me to suck in, as if someone had rid the universe of all of it and left me with lungs that wouldn't work.

I stumbled onto the small shoreline and watched the waves of Puget Sound wash across the rocky shore.

"Hey." One of the guys from before, the blond one, approached. "I'm Jenner."

He held out his hand.

I stared at it and then finally shook it. "Kartini."

"I know."

"Apparently, everyone does." I crossed my arms.

"You alone?"

I frowned. "Uh, no. There're like a billion people at this wedding."

He chuckled and tossed back the rest of his beer then set the bottle on the shore. "Nah, I mean out here…"

Goosebumps rose all over my body when I realized just how far I'd run—the music would drown out my screams. I'd left my heels, which meant I only had the knife I kept strapped to my thigh. And even then, he'd see me reach for it.

"I'm waiting for my boyfriend," I lied. One thing about the mafia, the parents taught us how to lie very well at an early age. "He was grabbing us more drinks. So, basically, that's a no. I will not make out with you, Jenner."

He threw back his head and laughed as if it were the funniest thing in the world. "I heard you were cute…pristine…untouched, but I had no idea how funny."

"I'm hilarious," I deadpanned. "Now, leave before my boyfriend rips your head from your body."

"I wonder…" He started to circle me.

"Fine, I'll play." I crossed my arms. "What? What do you wonder?"

His fingertip traced across my shoulder and around my neck to my other bare shoulder. My navy-blue strapless dress suddenly felt like too little clothing as he moved to stand behind me. "I wonder how good it'll feel to rip this dress from your body while nobody hears you scream."

I tried not to shake. "Your funeral, Jenner, your funeral."

"You don't have a boyfriend," he whispered in my ear, placing his hands on my shoulders and gripping them tightly. "And nobody's going to hear because you won't be alive when it's happening. Think of it as a parting gift. That I'll kill you before I fuck you."

My legs wobbled. "Go home, Jenner, you're clearly drunk, and only sociopaths are into necrophilia."

His dark chuckle wasn't helpful at all as his hands continued roaming from my shoulders down my arms. "I think I can be into anything if it means I take out Sergio Abandonato's favorite daughter."

"So, this is a hit?" I hoped I sounded curious as I slid a shaking hand down the front of my dress and slowly started to hike it up.

"Imagine when your daddy finds you on the beach, dress ripped, virginity stolen—"

"Then don't let me die a virgin. If you're gonna kill me, you may as well send me off with a nice screw. That is unless your dick's tiny. And if that's the case, no thank you."

He shoved me forward. "You little bitch!"

I laughed, hoping to taunt him. "Oh, wow, so it *is* small? Is this your kink, then? You have to wait until the girls are dead so they don't point and laugh?"

"Shut your mouth!" he roared as I continued lifting my dress, inviting him to watch. His eyes were furious, but his jaw went slack when he saw what I was doing.

"Like what you see, tiny dick?"

"Say it again, and I won't do it."

I pouted. "Fine. Tell me how much you want me, gorgeous."

He grunted. "Better."

Men were idiots.

I sauntered toward him as he jerked off his tie then pulled his black trousers loose, taking himself in hand with a moan.

I nearly barfed as I smiled up at him. "That's hot…"

"You're not…"

"Yeah, too bad I'm about to be dead…cold…"

"I have to." He hissed out a grunt as I moved toward him and then gripped him with my hand, shoving his away. "Oh, shit…"

"Glad to be proven wrong…" I whispered. One hand worked him, and the other finally reached the holster around my upper thigh. I slowly slid my knife out.

His eyes popped open.

I gripped him harder.

He stumbled forward just as I pushed the tip of my blade toward his stomach and shoved, using the momentum of his body to get it in deep.

"Son of a bitch!" He slammed me away from him, my knife still sticking out of his gut as blood stained his hands. "I'm gonna kill you!"

He grabbed me by the hair. I kicked him in the thigh and then kneed him in his engorged dick before he slammed me back against the rocks.

He jerked out the knife and came at me.

I jumped to my feet and knew in that moment that every moment spent training with my dad at five in the morning and learning how to defend, how to kill, came down to this man and my life.

His smile flashed before my eyes.

My cousins' hurtful words came next.

And then Tank, calling me "little girl" as I shot toward Jenner and flipped myself around to his back, putting him in a chokehold as he tried to slam his body back against the rocks.

With each slam of rock digging into my skin, I held tighter.

And I screamed.

I screamed until my voice was hoarse.

And until he stopped moving.

And then I screamed some more, only to hear Maksim's voice.

"No, get away. I'll kill you! I'll kill you!" I yelled.

"Tiny!" Maksim peeled me away from Jenner and held me in his arms, bloody. "It's okay, it's okay, it's me, it's just me…calm down, he's dead…"

"H-he's dead? Are you sure?" I was shaking like a leaf as he held me close in his arms. "Are you sure?"

Maksim squeezed me harder and whispered, "You were fucking brilliant, Tiny."

Blood stained my hands.

Tears stained my cheeks.

I would have scars forever on the inside.

And on my back.

And I knew, in that moment, that I'd just gone from sitting at the kid's table to being made.

All before my time.

I'd killed Jenner.

And part of my innocence had died with him.

Chapter Two

Kartini

Present Day

"You look like shit." Izzy plopped down on my bed with her phone and yawned. How she managed to look completely put-together in nothing but knee-high boots and a long sweatshirt was truly beyond my comprehension. She made effortless look chic and flawless.

"Thanks, bitch." I smacked her on the ass then studied myself in the mirror. Sometimes, I still saw the blood on my hands.

Other times, I woke up with a choking sensation as Jenner promised to screw me after he killed me.

The worst was when I heard his dark chuckle, his voice still whispering my name as if he had a right to even conjure it from the pit of Hell.

Therapy hadn't worked. *Thanks, Dad. At least you tried.*

And acting out was the only thing that made me feel…alive.

Less dead.

Less like a disappointment.

God, that had been the worst day.

Truly the absolute worst of my existence.

And it wasn't just Jenner's death.

It was that he'd told. Maksim.

He'd told my dad. My hero. Mine.

Maksim had brought me to him.

No longer the perfect princess but broken, bruised, battered, used, even though my virginity was still intact at seventeen—yay, me.

I couldn't scratch the image of leaving him on that dance floor and then returning a failure from my mind. Even though he'd said he was proud of me, I could see the sadness in his eyes.

And it wasn't because I'd lived.

It was because he knew what I would have to live with for the rest of my life, and the fact that he knew only made it feel worse, like swallowing fire and staring at water but not being able to reach it.

Since then, I couldn't even look at him, my hero. Something had shifted, like I'd suddenly been altered, turned into this unsure villain despite my dad's encouragement to defend myself, kill, whatever was necessary.

And that's when I realized it.

Something I hadn't seen.

The one thing that was broken inside me.

My confidence.

Because all my life, my confidence had been in my Family, in my father, in our name, in what we did.

And in one moment, one horrible person had shattered that.

And no matter what I did...

How many times I changed my hair...

Took shots of whiskey...

Got high like I actually enjoyed it when it only ever made me feel numb to the darkness that always tried to close in on me when I was by myself...

I was sick.

Broken.

And I felt stupid that it was over something so...ridiculously dumb when you compared it to everyone else in our Family.

I mean, my cousins Junior and Serena were willing to die for each other.

Valerian had an entirely different identity and then seduced Violet out of pure love and need to keep her safe, only after seducing her as, um... well, not a nice guy.

And don't even get me started on Ash and Annie. The hate and the love were almost equal and yet it worked, you know, after he got over blaming her for his fianceé's death.

I groaned.

See?

I had no reason for the baggage.

No reason for comparing my story to my cousins'—comparing my suffering.

And yet, there the baggage sat, unchecked, dangling from my arms and legs.

Izzy was quiet for way too long.

Had I been in my head—yup, I had been because her crystal-blue eyes stared at me in comfort and support, through my reflection in the mirror.

"What do you see?" I asked, crossing my arms across my black Nike crop top. It left a few inches of skin visible before meeting my white, high-waisted leggings and blue Jordan high-tops.

"Welllll…" Izzy winked. "I think you look hot. But what's more than that…" Her face sobered briefly. "I think…no matter what you look like, you'll always feel lost."

Her eyes flickered away while mine turned down to my feet, to my brand-new expensive shoes, something that anyone nearly nineteen would kill for. And they were just shoes, footwear that hid something that was dying inside me.

Something that needed to be set free.

Something I couldn't identify.

Couldn't save.

"Look…" Izzy was suddenly behind me, her chin resting on my shoulder. "I love you, no matter what, Tiny. But I know something happened. I wish you'd trust me enough to tell me. The point in all of this is to find something that truly makes you happy. That makes…" Her eyes darted away and then back. "That makes you want to live. Do you think…you have that something?"

"You're just a little girl!"

"Am not!" I stomped on Tank's foot and then stormed off.

With a grin I hadn't felt in a year, I looked up into the mirror and smirked. "I think I know what would make me happy."

"Me?"

"No."

"Good, because that smile was starting to make me feel like I needed a security detail and an AK-47."

I laughed even harder. "He'll be fine."

"He?" Her eyebrows shot up. "Oh, wait, we're torturing someone?"

Now, she gets excited? Poor Maksim.

I rolled my eyes. "Not really. I'll just torture him for one lame day and get back to my life. But the fact that I can even get a rise out of him brings me joy, and you did say…what makes me happy?"

Her gorgeous, wide smile beamed as her jet-black hair bounced down to her ass like a friggin' Kardashian. "Absolutely."

"Good talk, Iz."

She blew a kiss toward me. "Good talk, Tiny."

I turned back to the mirror with an evil grin. If I couldn't be happy. Content. If I couldn't sleep. Why let him? After all, he was the one who'd gotten away, who didn't save me. Not that he'd heard me screaming, but I'd always imagined him coming in on a white horse.

Instead…

He'd done nothing.

Which was worse than rejecting me.

So, I'd make him pay, just a little. For his flirting and his constant attention before the incident—before the change.

I would make his life a living Hell.

Twenty-four hours.

Ha, strap up, princess, because Tiny is hella coming for Tank!

Chapter Three

Tank

I knocked on Director Thompsons' door.

"Come in." He didn't look up from his desk.

He was in his late fifties with salt and pepper hair and a constant scowl on his face as if the world couldn't help but disappoint him on a daily basis. Then again, if people saw what we did…

Lived how we did at the bureau, well…it was hard to find the light in things—the happy when everything seemed so dark and tragic.

"Yes." His brown eyes crinkled at the corners as he scanned me intently from the black folder he was holding. "This true?"

Shit.

"Well, that depends on what it says." I knew what those black folders meant. Had they finally forced my hand? Finally sent the FBI something that meant this would be my last day?

My badge burned in my pocket as I crossed my arms.

"Sit." He pointed to the cold metal chair.

I stalked over to it, trying to fit my giant frame into a tiny seat was hellishly uncomfortable. Maybe a few years ago, I would have been able to, but not since working out with Ash.

I'd thought Quantico was rough.

Ha, they should just send in Ash, Junior, King, Maksim, and Valerian. *That* would be tough.

They bled like they liked it.

They were grumpy when they weren't injured.

And I rarely saw them smile without at least some blood on their person.

I'd been forced to fight. Forced to lift more weights than I'd ever seen in my entire life, forced to live their life in order to survive.

I didn't feel sorry for myself.

I just felt bad for my sore ass as I moved on the chair and tried to get comfortable.

"You've changed," Thompsons said with a sigh. "I'd believe it with my own eyes even if I hadn't been sent this folder this morning."

"I'm assuming this is where you ask me to turn in my badge, gun, and—"

He held up his hand. "I just need to know if it's true."

"You'll have to be more specific."

"Are you made?" He leaned forward, clasping his hands together so tightly, his skin turned a palish white.

Shit.

He didn't know, then?

He'd seen the bruises on my face.

He'd seen the limps as I walked into the office.

He knew I was undercover.

Everyone assumed that I was working for one side but pretending to work for both.

They were wrong.

Because, somehow, the Five Families had become my family. Somehow, they'd healed me in a way the FBI never would and never could.

I was half De Lange, after all, wasn't I? Half-blood of the most hated mafia line in the entire universe. Yay.

Maybe that's why I chose the good guys, only to realize too late that both sides were good—both sides justified the spilling of blood.

But only one side was loyal to the death.

And it wasn't the one with the badge.

"Yes," I finally said. "I've been made."

His sigh was long and drawn out. "What the hell do you want me to do with this information, Tank?"

"Burn it?" I offered.

The lines on his forehead deepened. "So that's it, then? You go undercover too young, and now I lose you forever?"

"You have other informants. I'm easily replaceable."

He flinched. "How do you know that?"

"Because you would never just lay all your cards out on the table. Quite honestly, I think you have someone else in the Family, I just don't know who would be desperate enough to work with you the way I was."

He pounded his fist onto his desk. "I saved you!"

"I know," I said softly. "You saved a lot of us. You gave us purpose. You gave us a life. But now it's time for me to make my own choices."

"I knew you were too young when I sent you in undercover."

I shrugged. "I was already so old in my own head, you know that. I was forced to live a rough life, and you gave me an out. I'll never forget that."

"And yet…" His smile was sad. "You choose the bad guys."

"They aren't bad," I said defensively. "Just…misunderstood."

"Justified killing is misunderstood?"

"You tell me," I fired back.

He tossed the black file toward me. "One more job, and then I'll be taking that badge, son."

My eyebrows rose in surprise as I leaned forward and checked out the folder. It was me standing next to Kartini at Valerian's wedding last year.

God, she'd been so pretty that day.

And then she'd just disappeared on everyone after the scene with Ash. Fucking Ash. Thank God he was himself again and not such an asshole, though he still had his moments.

Annie, his girlfriend, balanced him like a pound of Xanax.

"Kartini Abandonato." I gulped. "What about her?"

"A few men in the field were killed that day. One of them was undercover for the Petrov Crime Family. I received his head in a cake box with a note signed: *xoxo, K.*"

I barked out a laugh. "Yeah, she would never do that."

"The daughter of a mobster? You sure?"

"Positive." But even as I said it, I knew something had shifted in her. But it had to be something other than chopping someone's head off. "What do you want me to do? I'm already her new babysitter for the next two weeks. So, if it's following her around, save the energy. It's already done."

He grinned. "Follow her. Befriend her. Get her to trust you. Seduce her." I flinched. "And find out what really happened to my men."

"You mean other than death?"

"Very funny."

"It wasn't meant to be."

He sighed again. "Tank, it's your last assignment. Keep it clean, get as close to her as possible. She's your new job."

"Great. So, both bosses want me to follow the terrifying Tiny Abandonato...what could go wrong?"

He frowned down at the picture. "You're literally three times her size."

"You haven't seen her balls."

His face cracked into a small smile. "Wait, are you...afraid of her?"

"Hell no!"

"Sure, okay."

"Can I be excused now?"

"Are you ten?"

I growled and shot to my feet. "Last job, and then I'm out."

"And then you'll...do what? Stay permanently at Sergio Abandonato's compound? Become a captain? Underboss? What?"

I was silent. And then... "I like his compound. It has a theater room."

"You used to hate pulling your gun," he said softly. "And now, it almost seems like you can't wait to use it."

"Yeah, well, if you'd seen what I have." I nodded. "You'd feel the same way...blood protects blood, sir. And no matter how many badges or awards you give me, nothing will change that."

Something that almost seemed like respect flickered in his eyes as he nodded and whispered, "You can go."

I left the black folder on his desk and ignored all the whispers and stares I received as I stomped through the offices.

I was rarely there, and when I was, people always talked about the guy who the FBI had somehow allowed to switch sides.

But I knew something they didn't.

A very long time ago, they'd had two FBI agents in the Five Families working for them.

Phoenix Nicolasi.

And Sergio himself.

So...they could judge me all they wanted.

Because they had no idea that the Five Families were on the fucking government payroll.

Idiot sheep.

I slammed the door to the offices behind me and groaned when I saw Giana Lang waiting in front of the elevator.

If Kartini was Satan's mistress, then Giana was the spawn of Satan. Her jet-black hair was pulled into a tight, severe bun, and the only color on her body was her trademark pink lipstick that always made her lips look too big, as if her mouth were just waiting to devour its next victim.

Her green eyes flashed when I went and stood next to her. I had no other choice at that point.

"I don't trust you," she said it as if she were bored.

"And I don't care." I shoved my hands into my jeans' pockets. "But your concern is noted."

She tapped her boring black heel against the concrete floor. "You're in too deep, Tank. And one day, the water's going to drown you."

I sighed. "Pretty sure the mafia will throw me a life jacket—they need me too much."

"That's where you're wrong." Something flashed behind her green eyes. "They don't need you. You need them."

"Excuse me?" Okay, now I was getting pissed. What the hell was her problem?

"That. Right there." She jutted a finger in my direction then tapped it once against my chest. "You're emotional about it. You're defensive in every meeting, and now you think you can just walk away from the bureau and set up camp with criminals and nobody's going to bat an eyelash? You're wrong, Tank. God, I can't believe they gave you a promotion last year."

"Still stings, doesn't it?" I grinned knowingly. "To know that no matter how many bad guys you arrest, I'll still be the favorite."

"I hate you."

"You hate yourself," I spat.

The elevator doors opened as I ignored her and grabbed my cell, dialing Sergio right in front of her like it didn't matter because, quite honestly, it didn't.

"What's up?" He sounded way too calm for a Tuesday.

"New assignment just happens to be your daughter. Know anything about that?"

"New assignment?"

I hesitated and noticed that Giana had gotten onto the elevator with me. Whatever. Let her hear. "Last assignment."

Out of the corner of my eye, I could have sworn she smiled.

"So, you've made your choice?"

"Did I ever really have one?" I snorted out a laugh.

He was quiet and then said, "We always have a choice."

"Sure, okay, tell that to all the rivers of blood we seem to bathe in."

Giana snorted out a humorless laugh next to me like she actually understood the double life I'd been living.

I rolled my eyes and whispered to her, "I was kidding. It was a metaphor."

"Sure, you were."

"Scaring small children again?" Sergio laughed.

"If only it worked on yours," I fired back.

"She's no longer a child, Tank."

Yeah, I knew. That was the problem.

Seven-year age difference.

Seven-year age difference.

I just kept repeating it to myself so I didn't feel like a total idiot and creeper.

"You're awfully quiet." He interrupted my mental chant. "And she's at the house. She was asking for you, actually."

"Oh, good, let the torture begin."

"Yours or hers?"

"Guess."

His laughter was all I heard before the line went dead.

The elevator doors opened, and Giana stepped out ahead of me, only to stop once she was in the hall. She called over her shoulder, "I hope you know what you're doing, Tank. Because it's not just your life you have to worry about."

"They can take care of themselves," I said calmly.

"We'll see," was all she said, leaving me wondering why her words felt more like a veiled threat than a dig.

Our conversation bothered me the entire drive to Sergio's.

And I had no idea why.

Chapter Four

Kartini

The door slammed.

"Honey, I'm home..." I said to myself with a grin.

I had a bottle of wine out on the living room table, my shoes on the glass as I leaned back and took a swig from my goblet—because why not get fancy at two in the afternoon?

"It's ten a.m," came Tank's annoyed voice.

Or ten in the morning...whoops.

"I don't own a watch." I shrugged.

"What's that on your left wrist, then?"

"Oh, that?" I shrugged. "It's an Apple watch used strictly for heart rate and exercise purposes."

"Exercise to you is opening your mouth and closing it, Tiny." He made it farther into the room, and I tried...I really did. I tried not to check him out.

Not to stare at his golden skin.

His bulging biceps beneath his plain black t-shirt.

The new ink poking out from the V of that same shirt.

Would he get the Abandonato crest like the rest of the Family?

I shivered.

He would look so hot with it across his chest.

Our crest.

Mine.

I shifted my eyes away too slowly, and he caught them with his green-eyed gaze before he licked his full lips like he saw something else he wanted to lick.

He always looked at me that way—with both annoyance and need.

And I never knew how to take it.

On one hand, I wanted to believe the need trumped any annoyance he felt for me, but I knew how he saw me.

As a spoiled brat with a silver spoon stuck up her ass.

And even worse now that I was older.

Now that I was…different.

"You added more blue." He jutted his chin toward me and sat down on the chair across from the sofa I was lying on.

"Yup." I examined my black nail polish. "I felt like it wasn't making a strong enough statement."

He snorted out a laugh. "And what sort of statement were you going for? Gothic chic?"

"What?" I glared at him. "You don't like it."

"It's not you."

Disappointment threatened to choke me, and shame crawled up my neck by way of a harsh red flush. "You don't know me."

"I did." He locked eyes with me. "Or I thought I did."

"People change, Tank."

"Not that dramatically." He saw too much. I needed to pester him, to get him to verbally spar or maybe just spar in general.

I shot to my feet. "Wanna fight?"

He groaned into his hands, his golden-brown hair falling forward over his forehead. "You ask this every week, and every week what do I tell you?"

"Ummm, no. You say 'no,' even though you know I can hold my own. I'm an Abandonato, so…" I walked right up to where he was sitting and kicked him in the shin.

"Son of a bitch, Tiny!" He roared in pain. "Why?"

I laughed. "Because you were being a pussy."

He glared. "Why are you like this?"

"Why are *you*?"

"What?"

"So…" I leaned down and whispered, "Weak."

That did it.

A barely controlled rage burned behind his green gaze as he jumped to his feet and picked me up like I weighed nothing, then tossed me over his shoulder and stomped toward the weight room.

I could barely contain my triumphant grin—until he bypassed the weight room and shoved me into my room, then started to close the door after tossing me onto my bed.

"Oh, hell no." I bolted after him just as the door caught my foot.

He glared. "Naptime, princess."

"You bastard!" I roared, clawing at his arm.

He shoved me back again, as gently as he probably could.

So, I jumped around onto his back.

He let out a roar and threw me back onto the bed, pinning my body beneath his as his chest heaved in exertion. "You drew blood."

"Where?" I laughed.

"My neck. And you're insane. You know that, right?"

I located the blood and very slowly lifted my head until my lips pressed against his neck. "There…" They vibrated against his skin. "All better."

He cursed under his breath. "We need ground rules."

"For?" I leaned back as he pulled his hands away.

"This." He growled. "No kissing me. No touching me. No annoying the hell out of me. Your dad put your safety in my hands for the wedding."

I let out a huff of embarrassment. "And why can't I touch you? Does it make you uncomfortable?" I trailed a finger from his neck down to the V of his shirt then gave it a small tug. "Hmmm?"

His lips parted as his expression shuddered, kicking me out of whatever emotions he refused to share with me. "Don't push me, Tiny. Not right now."

"See, I think that's exactly what you need, Tank…to let me shove you right off that cliff into oblivion. Think how good it would feel."

He jerked away from me. "Yes, and then decapitation by way of your father, all in the name of you having a bit of fun with my life. No, thank you." He growled. "We leave Friday morning. Get your shit packed."

"Already am." I shrugged. It was a first, considering I'd never packed a week before anything—I was that excited.

"You?"

I nodded toward my Louis Vuitton luggage.

"I'm almost afraid to ask what you packed for the Mexico trip," he admitted, which earned a laugh out of me.

"Oh, Tank, it's a surprise."

"Was afraid you were going to say that," he grumbled and then shot me a glare. "Promise me you at least brought...underwear of some sort."

I fluttered my eyelashes. "Why are you suddenly so concerned with my underwear?"

He clenched his teeth, his jaw ticking with annoyance. "Because it's my job to make sure you don't end up pregnant at eighteen, and flashing men your goods just to piss me off sounds like the sort of thing you'd call 'fun.'"

"Cute air quotes." I laughed. "And I guess you'll find out."

"Another sleepless night, how wonderful," he grumbled.

"Dream of me, old man."

His answer was a middle finger as he walked out of my room and slammed the door.

Of course, he didn't see how my smile fell.

Or how I suddenly felt as empty on the inside as my room felt without him in it.

Why him of all people?

I was happy when he was near.

And then, when he was gone, I had this longing, and it pissed me off that somehow Tank was connected to it.

Then again, he'd always been connected.

I kicked my suitcase and then flopped back onto the bed.

Mexico.

With Tank as my babysitter.

Which meant he was forced to be in my presence—didn't choose to be.

It also meant I only had another few weeks by his side before he made a choice—the Family or the FBI.

With a grin, I jumped up and unzipped my suitcase, then promptly tossed all my underwear onto my bed and zipped my bag back up.

Sorry, not sorry, Tank.

Let the games begin.

Chapter Five

Tank

"Mexicoooooooo!" Junior shouted once we were all in the black SUVs that had been waiting at the private airstrip for the G-V I was on to land. Altogether, we took three of the jets. I still wasn't over the fact that each of the Families had their own jets. Yes, plural. Jets.

Thirty-million-dollar jets.

I'd looked it up.

Then promptly tried to forget how much a luxury like that cost. The last thing I needed to know was just how illegally rich they were and why.

"Dude." Ash shoved Junior and then wrapped an arm around Annie. It still made my teeth clench.

I knew they were right for each other.

But at one point last year, I had thought Annie would eventually see that he was toxic, that he couldn't love, and that our friendship could turn into something more.

Then the asshat had to come in and confuse her with all his feelings bleeding all over the place like a continuously erupting volcano.

Again, I got it.

I was okay with it.

But that didn't mean I enjoyed watching him basically devour her face in front of me as he pulled her into his lap and started whispering what I could only guess were sexual innuendos in her ear as she blushed beet-red. Her hair was growing longer, another sign that she was his since she'd cut it to piss him off.

"Wonder what they're going to do once they get to the hotel," Tiny said without looking up from her phone, while Maksim laughed behind her, only to earn a glare from Izzy as if he weren't allowed to think about sex unless it was with her.

Damn awkward breakup that one was.

Yet again, it reminded me why all the bosses had told the kids that they weren't allowed to date.

It only created drama.

I put on my black Ray-Bans and waited for the arguing to start. The kids, even though they weren't kids and almost all in their early twenties, did nothing but bicker, tease, fight—it was a true family. All the bosses were nice enough to let us stick together in our own private villa while they stayed across the hotel in another with the younger siblings.

Which meant I would have zero backup when it came to Tiny.

Serena clinked her chilled glass of champagne with Junior as they locked eyes across their seats. "You ready?"

He licked his lips. "I was ready to marry you at sixteen."

"And here we go," King said from the front seat as he flipped around with a scowl. "You know some of us aren't getting regular sex, sooo if you guys could just—"

"Wait!" Maksim gripped the leather seat. "You stopped seeing your tutor?"

It was Valerian, his adopted brother's turn to snicker. "Dad said, and I quote, 'I will pull your liver through your pee hole if you keep fucking your twenty-five-year-old tutor,' or something like that."

"Very specific." Maksim whistled with a cheeky grin. "Huh, King?"

King flipped the entire van off and lifted his chin in defiance. "I'll have you know she was my first love."

Everyone burst out laughing—me included.

"Bullshit! You're eighteen!" Ash called him out.

"Um, Valerian's twenty-one, you're twenty, and all of our parents got married when they were young, thus all of them still looking like they belong on a calendar."

"That was creepy, bro, just saying." Maksim shuddered.

"Agreed," I grumbled.

All eyes fell to me. "What? Look, yes, your parents are attractive—wait a second, why the hell are we having this conversation?"

Ash burst out laughing. "Tank, I say this with love, but I'll probably choke you if you decide to choose the FBI instead of us…" He grinned. "All in favor…"

Everyone raised their hands but Tiny.

Shocker.

Izzy elbowed her.

She looked up from her phone. "What?"

"Cold-hearted Abandonato girls…" Maksim just shook his head. "The only females that terrify me."

Izzy waved at him.

He paled and looked away.

"What's so important that you can't participate in adult time, Tiny?" Ash asked.

"TikTok," was her cold response. "Some guys reacting to my favorite mac and cheese recipes."

"*Wow*," Junior mouthed in my direction.

Serena shared a look with me that I couldn't decipher and then whispered something to Junior.

His face fell a bit.

Shit, were they talking about her?

Again?

Everyone wanted to reach her.

Nobody could.

It was pointless to even try.

She had every single guard up that she could find.

And as far as I knew, nobody had apologized for last year. I was sure she knew why Ash had lashed out, but that didn't make it any less painful or embarrassing. The feeling of not belonging with the people you loved the most.

They pretended like it didn't happen.

But I still felt the elephant in the room, which pissed me off because that meant I wanted to defend the devil.

The van pulled up to a huge resort that I knew probably cost more than my yearly paycheck to stay at. There was a long line of hotel staff waiting for us at the front with more trays of champagne.

I wasn't used to this sort of extravagance, so I just followed the guys when they all started piling the luggage outside the van.

I'd never been to Cabo—it wasn't like I was dripping with money from the FBI. If anything, I almost felt guilty that this was part of my job, following the terrifying girl who had me by the balls without even realizing it…and trying like hell to figure out how to crack that same scary façade in order to gain intel.

Seducing her just seemed like a really easy way to get castrated while on vacation.

Then again, sometimes, she stared.

I wasn't sure if it was because she found me attractive or if she was just curious by nature at what the hell an FBI spy was still doing at her house, helping.

"Here you go." Ash held out a tip to one of the bellmen.

I nearly choked when I noticed it was two hundred-dollar bills.

The bellman said, "Thank you," refusing to look down, and then a lady in an all-white uniform smiled brightly at us. She had red lipstick, curly brown hair, and curves I knew King was already memorizing since Maksim smacked him on the back of the head when she turned around, showing a tight ass.

"What?" King rubbed his head. "I was appreciating Cabo!"

"Appreciate the birds." Maksim gave him a hard shove and pointed skyward.

"Like you should talk. Literally every guy in this family's a manwhore. It's like a badge of honor!"

Izzy snorted.

Serena glared at Junior as if he were cheating. He held up his hands. "Thanks, guys."

And Ash just reached for Annie's hand and kissed it.

Maybe my hell wasn't Tiny.

Perhaps it was watching all the happy couples while I tried to stay alive and keep the small one from getting drunk off her ass.

I tried not to look too stunned as I followed the group around the property. There were seven pools—that I could see.

A gorgeous blue ocean that didn't look real to the naked eye, and a sunset that instantly relaxed me.

I glanced around and dumbly wondered why I didn't see that many guests. In fact, I didn't see *any* guests.

Only staff.

At least a dozen restaurants that were nearly empty.

I elbowed Ash. "Why is it so deserted?"

He grinned. It honestly freaked me out how much he smiled now. Then again, he was in love, half-healed, though still half-monster if you crossed him. "It's ours."

"Ours," I repeated. "As in yours? Like you rented it all out?"

"No." He shrugged. "Ours, as in my dad owns it."

"The senator? Chase? Your dad?" I gaped. "Owns this?"

"What can I say?" Ash said. "He likes nice things." When I didn't answer, Ash just whispered, "Close your mouth, bro, and try to enjoy it. You deserve it after all the times I kicked your ass in the ring this last year and all the times in the future I will make you bleed."

"Comforting," I grumbled.

"I try." He patted me on the back and then whispered something to Annie.

Kartini was on my other side, her giant Prada sunglasses perched high on her face. Her lips were pressed together in a scowl, and her hand clutched her purse so tightly, I wondered if she was upset about something.

"You all right?" I asked as we turned another corner.

"Huh? What?" She looked up at me. "Sorry, was daydreaming…"

"Yeah, I look scared shitless when I daydream, too," I said under my breath. "You know, if you ever need to talk—"

"Ah, a babysitter and a therapist, how'd I get so lucky?"

"You don't have to be a bitch," I hissed. "God, I was just trying to help."

"I don't need your help."

"Clearly," I muttered. "Look, I'll do my damn job while here, but let's just try to keep as much space between us as possible."

"Agreed," she sneered.

"Fine." I felt like a toddler.

"Great." Her smile was syrupy-sweet, all white teeth and bright red lipstick.

I nearly collided with Ash's back when we all stopped.

"We're so happy you've come back to NC Resort and Spa."

"NC?" I muttered.

"Nixon, Chase, one of their many joint ventures." Maksim piped up. "Oh, look, the bungalow…" And then, with a sprint, he held out his hand to the woman. "Can I have that one, pleasssssseeee?"

She gaped and then handed him a room key. "Wait for me!" King chased after him.

"Oh no, you don't!" Izzy squealed, grabbing her own keycard and jogging after them toward a gorgeous beach bungalow with a treehouse located right on the water.

Screaming ensued.

I could have sworn I heard a gunshot go off—and let's be honest, it probably did—as they took over the beach bungalow.

Hell, Maksim better sleep with one eye open—or both...both would be better.

"Honeymoon Suite." Junior stepped up and held out his hand.

And they were off.

Ash and Annie followed suit.

Then Valerian and Violet.

Leaving...

Yup, you guessed it.

Me and Satan's mistress.

"The last bungalow." The woman beamed. "It's one of my favorites. You can see the sunset every night." Goody. "Besides, you two look like you won't be venturing outside a lot anyway. I know these things."

I barely contained my sputter of denial when Kartini leaned against me and straight-up petted my chest with her dangerously long fingernails. "Aw, you could tell?"

"Lots of sexual tension. Your auras are..." She shuddered. "I've never seen anything like it."

"Yes, well..." Tiny's fingernails raked down the front of my shirt. Holy shit, was she ripping it open? "I would be so lost without my big, bad, sexy bodyguard." She smacked my ass. "Have you seen this hunk?"

The woman blushed. "I'm Michelle. If you need anything, please don't hesitate to call the concierge number on your phone."

"Perrrfect." Kartini took a keycard. "Actually, can you have a bottle of Patron sent to the room along with a deck of playing cards? Oh, and a bottle of Dom Perignon."

And here we go!

"Oh, and cigars," she added. "Oh, wait, do you have blow—?"

"Holy shit, Kartini," I ground out. "That's illegal."

"It's Mexico."

"FBI agent," I reminded her.

Michelle's eyes widened.

"Don't worry," Kartini grinned. "He's kind of stuck with us, so even if you do have other party drugs, he'll be quiet. Won't you, Tank?"

I just shook my head. "If you die, I die. So, no, I won't be quiet." I turned back to Michelle. "No drugs, she's barely legal drinking age here as it is. Just the alcohol and some Advil."

"Awww, baby, did the trip give you a migraine?" Kartini clung to my biceps with both hands.

"Yes. The trip. Of course, what else could it be?" I glared down at the tiny, insane human. "Let's go." I grabbed my keycard, and off we went as Michelle grinned after us like we hadn't just asked for illegal drugs fifteen minutes into our trip.

"Unbelievable," I ground out as I slid the card across the black pad on the door three minutes later. "Are you seriously doing drugs now? Be honest because I won't stand for it. I won't, Kartini. That's a hard limit, a fucking hard limit, and not a road you want to travel down. People don't just quit and come back up, and they don't just—" I stopped talking when I realized she wasn't interrupting me, rubbing up against me, trying to kill me.

It was unnerving.

I didn't know how to handle it when she was quiet.

She jerked off her sunglasses. "Is this your protective old-man way of saying you care about what happens to me?"

"Fuck." I spread my arms wide. "Why else would I be here? Risking my life every day to keep you safe? For fun? Do you think I enjoy being your dad's target practice?"

"Oh, get over it, Tank. That was one time!"

"It was fucking terrifying!" I roared while she laughed into her hands. Her eyes were glassy, and she quickly looked away. "Hey…what's going on?"

She sighed, and part of the façade slipped. "This used to be our thing."

"Who?"

"Me and Dad." She stared out at the balcony. "We would come here every year for my birthday. I'd dance on his feet after dinner. He'd read me stories about princesses in big towers and knights who fought to win their love. Their hearts."

"Did it stop?" I asked, suddenly curious, unable to look away from the wistful look reflected in her face as she stared at the ocean.

She gulped, her blue eyes glassy. "It had to. People grow up, Tank."

I crossed my arms. "Just because you grow up doesn't mean you stop needing to hear stories about love and hope. You'll be ninety and still smiling when the prince earns the princess's good favor. You'll be a hundred and still smile at a first kiss. You'll die knowing you were loved, and loved in the very best way. So, no, you don't just grow out of it, Tiny."

She gasped—it was slight—and then she awkwardly mumbled

something about unpacking.

And I was left wondering what the hell had happened between the wedding and this year, and even more curious how involved she was with the death of that FBI agent.

Guilt pounded like a freaking heartbeat against my chest when I thought about that day.

About what had gone down.

And what hadn't.

Did they know?

Was that the reason the Families accepted me?

Because when it came time to choose—I chose them.

And protected her in really the only way I knew how.

By grabbing a drink with her, by talking, flirting, and for one fucking moment going…*it's okay to like her, to find her attractive. It's okay to feel possessive.*

It would be okay.

I let out a groan.

Clearly, the only thing that had just broken was a wall, even slightly. Okay, so I made a scratch against it, but it was still a scratch.

Hell.

I had to be nice.

Like really nice.

I had to be vulnerable to possibly the only girl who could hurt me, who could stomp all over my heart with her stilettos and laugh while doing it.

Once she was out of earshot, I dialed Ash's number, the one person I knew I could trust and who wouldn't actually kill me dead for what I was about to say.

"Kinda busy…" he groaned into the phone. So, they wasted no time.

"I figured." I peered around the living room entrance to make sure Tiny wasn't creeping back up on me like a bad nightmare. "Look, I need you to help me seduce Kartini, but in a way where my dick stays intact, her father doesn't shoot me in the face then rip my dick off and feed it to me, and she doesn't get hurt."

He was silent.

"Ash?"

"Are you shitting me right now?"

I groaned. "Yes, because I just love interrupting sexy times with my two friends just so I can shit with you. Look, I'll tell you later why, just know that, right now, my last job before I join this little funhouse you guys call a Family is to find something out. And the only way I can do that is to get closer to her. And, right now, she looks ready to impale me with all ten fingernails."

"Dangerous game, bro." Ash sighed. "Fine, give us five minutes, then get your ass over here."

I whistled. "Only five? Ash, I'm fucking disappointed."

"Ha!" I could almost see him flipping me off. "Trust me, she won't be. I can't help it if I please her so fast, she sees stars before I'm even ready to—"

"Yup, yup, good talk. Gotta go."

I hung up to his laughter.

And most likely her moans.

I shuddered and then checked my watch.

Five minutes.

And I was going to her cousin for intel.

And telling him the whole story of why I needed her.

But leaving out the part where I actually admitted that I never stopped wanting her for the last year.

With every stolen look.

Every fight.

Every scowl.

I'd wanted her.

I'd just have to shove that want deep down and do my job so I could get out of the FBI alive.

And into the Family—my family. For good.

I mean, how hard could it be?

"Hey, ass face," Kartini called. "Our tequila here yet?"

I groaned and fell face-first onto the couch, only to feel a slap against my ass, then another as she sat on me and sighed. "Why are they so slow?"

"Ask God." I moaned into a pillow.

And nearly groaned when her hand found my ass again, this time to squeeze.

Maybe seduction wouldn't be so hard, after all.

On her.

But for me?

That was another matter entirely.

Chapter Six

Kartini

I expected to get drunk, listen to music on the beach, and maybe have a one-night stand.

Instead, I was trying not to stare at Tank while he did pushups two hours later in the living room and nearly died when a bead of sweat ran down the middle of his back and into his dark Nike shorts.

His muscles had muscles. He was every girl's fantasy wrapped up in one sexually pent-up package.

I may have licked my lips when he groaned and flipped onto his back for situps—damn those abs. Damn them to hell because…just…damn.

I reached for him like an idiot, my fingertips flinching at my sides as if they needed something to hold onto, and that something was all eight abs.

Then berated myself for being tempted.

He hadn't come to save me.

He came to watch over me.

To keep me safe.

"Too late," I wanted to say. Even though I knew it wasn't his fault, I had to blame someone.

And I blamed him.

I blamed him as much as I wanted him.

It was a serious problem.

I stared at the shot glass in my hand and then tossed it back. "When's dinner?"

"Am I your chef now, too?" he grunted from the floor.

I gulped, swallowing against a very dry throat. "No, G.I Joe..." I had to look away again. "I mean, when's Family dinner? We always do Family dinner the first night."

He jumped to his feet and grabbed a towel. "Looks like most everyone is getting room service."

My heart dropped.

Why was I being like this?

I'd been excited for Cabo because the last time I'd been here had been right before the wedding. Things had felt normal, perfect.

I'd been normal.

Perfect.

And I'd thought...I just thought that maybe it would be healing.

And now, I was sad.

A bit heartbroken.

Oh, I knew if I called my dad, he'd be here in a heartbeat. But I also knew he and Mom needed a break, and I was a grown-ass adult.

Who, apparently, still needed way too many hugs and too much attention.

I didn't hear Tank's approach until he grabbed the phone next to the lamp right where I was sitting and picked it up. "Yes, reservations for dinner in thirty minutes..." His eyes met mine. "Italian sounds good. Yes, for two. Thanks."

He hung up.

And I stared like a woman completely lost.

And maybe halfway unhinged.

"We can just have room service," I blurted.

His smile was lethal, too pretty to be real as he leaned in and whispered, "Now, where's the fun in that?"

I couldn't breathe. "Y-you're being tolerable. It's terrifying. Why?"

"Because."

"Tank—"

"Can't you just say 'thank you' and drop it?"

"Absolutely not," I blurted.

He groaned and ran both hands through his hair in what I could only assume was frustration. "Because you sounded sad, and it fucks with me when you sound sad, okay? Happy?" He threw the towel against the floor and then picked it up, mumbling, "Wear underwear."

I gulped.

Because I didn't have any thanks to my insanely horrible idea back when he'd pissed me off for the millionth time in Chicago.

And he'd think I was doing it to annoy him.

I'd just have to lie.

Knowing that he would be wondering if I listened the entire time.

My body shivered.

This was either a really bad idea or the best I'd ever had.

Dinner alone with a guy I'd wanted, then hated, only to want him again and need to hate so I felt better about myself.

The enemy.

An FBI agent, for crying out loud.

My friggin' bodyguard!

I mean, why did I need protection in the first place?

Then again, I had been rebelling a lot lately. But I just…wanted to feel—something, anything!

Tank poked his head back around the corner. "Wear white."

"H-huh?" I jumped in my seat. "Why?"

His eyes locked on mine. "Because you look really pretty in white, and because I said so."

I stuck out my tongue.

"Do it again. I dare you." He growled, eyes flashing toward my mouth as his nostrils flared as if he could smell my lust—feel my need crackling through the night air.

My stomach fluttered. Normally, I would have taunted him. This time, I decided he looked too predatory.

So, I just gulped and said, "You're lucky I brought a white dress."

"You're lucky you get to keep it on," he said before disappearing, leaving my mouth gaping open and my cheeks hot.

What in the ever-loving hell was going on?

And why did I like it so much?

Was he finally noticing me?

Or was this a game?

An angle?

Trust no one but Family.

But he was half-De Lange.

So, technically, family within the Five Families, though not related to me.

Could I trust him, though? *Really* trust him?

My dad had assigned him to me.

Repeatedly.

But he'd never once crossed that line.

Which begged the question…

Why now?

* * * *

"This is nice." My voice was low as Tank helped me into my chair. A bottle of champagne was already opened and waiting for us when we got there.

And we had the entire restaurant to ourselves.

If I were a romantic, I'd say it was a date.

But we owned the place. Ergo, it was empty because we paid for it to be that way, and it wasn't Tank who'd done it.

"Champagne?" our waiter asked.

"Yes, please." I held up my flute.

He poured some into both of our glasses then introduced himself. "I'm Marco. I'll be your server the entire night. Please take your time looking over the menu and drop your red napkin to the floor when you're in need of me."

That was new.

And this could get fun very fast.

I grinned. "Perfect."

Tank gave me a warning stare across his menu and mouthed my name as if to scold me before I even did anything!

Marco turned.

I grabbed my napkin.

Then Tank grabbed my wrist. "Behave."

"I was going to put it on my lap."

"Bullshit"—he laughed—"you were going to drop it about a million times so poor Marco got his cardio in for the year."

I sucked my lower lip. "Am I that transparent? Damn."

"No." His smile was deadly. "I just know you too well…remember? The old man who follows you around, that you use as a human shield?"

"Aw, you'd die for me?" I teased.

He sobered. "Without a second thought."

Had I been holding my fork, it would have clattered against my plate only to tumble to the floor. "Because I'm your job, right? Because my dad would kill you for not protecting me?"

Please say, "no."

Please say it's because you couldn't live with yourself.

Who was I kidding? He barely tolerated me.

"I don't like that look," Tank whispered.

"Huh? What?" I forced a smile.

"The one you just wore that looked defeated, sad. I hate it. I've only ever seen it a handful of times because I'm pretty sure you practice your perfect smiles so nobody sees beneath whatever you're trying to hide, but I see it. I see you." My breath hitched. My heart pounded against my chest. "And I don't like that look." He paused and leaned forward, his muscled forearms resting against the white tablecloth, his tanned skin glowing in the candlelight. "And I'd die for you, yes, because you're my job." I deflated immediately. "But also because this world would be a very sad place without Satan's mistress in it."

I choked on my laugh. "Nice."

"I thought so." He winked. "At least, you're smiling again."

I swallowed back the feminine squeak threatening to burst from my lips and said, "I smile."

"Sometimes," he said cryptically, his lips pressed into a knowing smile that had me shifting in my chair. "So..." He pulled up the large, red menu again. "Do you know what you want?"

"Hamburger," I said without even looking at the menu. "And fries. All the fries. Extra pickles. And I'd probably choke you for a taco."

He shot me a stunned expression. "You're in a super-expensive Italian restaurant, and you're thinking about choking me for a taco? Who are you?"

I beamed. "Expensive restaurants never give enough food. I'll order lasagna and end up eating seven plates of it before I'm full. But when you order American food at an Italian restaurant, it's almost like they remember how big we like our serving sizes."

He started to laugh. It was gorgeous on him. *He* was gorgeous. *Focus, Kartini, focus.* "I oddly get that." My fingers itched to grab the napkin and drop it. After a few seconds, he rolled his eyes. "Fine, fine, drop the damn napkin."

"YAY!" I grabbed it and threw it onto the floor with glee. Best part of my night so far; well, that and the small dimple on the right side of Tank's cheek.

Why did he have to be so damn sexy?

Why did his hair have to have this natural wave to it that looked too perfect to be real?

Marcus came power-walking over. "Have you decided?"

"More champagne." I grinned. "And I'd like a burger, fries, and the calamari."

"With a stroke on the side," Tank added, grinning up at me. "Actually, I'll have the same thing, but can we get a cannoli, too?"

Marcus wrote it all down. "Great choices."

When he left, Tank leaned in. "If I end up in the hospital with a stomachache and an inability to digest, I blame you."

"Aww, poor baby, just hydrate. You'll be fine." I winked. "Besides, the alcohol will help digestion. It's science."

He barked out a laugh. "Um, no, actually it's not. But it's cute that you think so."

"I'm cute." I winked.

He choked on his sip of champagne. "Maybe cute's too tame of a word."

"Feisty?"

He tapped his glass against mine. "Better."

We ate and talked the entire time.

I couldn't remember having a better dinner.

And it helped me forget.

He helped me forget.

Like he knew I needed to get out of the hotel room, needed to feel normal even though he had no clue why I didn't.

We were both a little tipsy as we walked back to the suite, and I loved that every time I stumbled into him, his arm moved a little bit more around me, keeping me close to him—keeping me safe.

I gave him a sloppy shrug once we were close to the shore and our room, then yelled, "Tag, you're it!"

Adrenaline propelled me toward the water.

And the need for someone to chase me—to catch me—sobered me up.

He stumbled across the sand in an effort to grab me as I peeled my cocktail dress over my naked body and went diving into the ocean. The warm waves had covered me by the time he chased after me, already pulling his shirt over his massive chest and gorgeous, lickable eight-pack.

"Wanna swim?" I called as normally as I could when staring at male perfection and that gorgeous body.

"Like I have a choice!" he yelled right back, throwing his shoes into the sand and shrugging out of his pants with jerky movements that had me hypnotized.

I told myself I wouldn't look.

But the champagne said it was an excellent idea as he dropped his briefs and gave me a scalding smirk that basically said: *"Look your fill."*

And I was rewarded because, apparently, every inch of him was huge.

And there were a lot of…inches.

I licked my salty lips and waited for him to dive in.

I wondered how he tasted.

I wondered if he'd push me away or let me sink my mouth onto him with wild abandon.

And then I wondered how tipsy I really was for even thinking about asking him if I could put my mouth on every hot inch of his body.

"See, aren't you so happy you agreed to skinny-dip?" I grinned once he broke the surface in typical Tank fashion—with a gorgeous scowl on his lips and intense eye contact that made me want to flick him on the nose and dive back under the water.

God, his stares were punishing.

Punish. Me.

My body pounded.

My pulse raced.

I ached.

He jerked me against him. "Sometimes, I think you have a death wish." His green eyes flashed. "We're both way beyond buzzed, in an ocean, with predators—"

"Meh, I only see one predator."

Another wave crashed, sending me into his naked arms.

He was so big.

So warm.

I shivered and then wrapped my legs around his waist, feeling the steely rod of his length pressed against me.

His eyes briefly closed as his jaw flexed. "You trying to get me killed?"

"Oh, please, my dad can't shoot this far in the dark."

"Yes, let's test that theory," he ground out.

"Well, your ass was pretty white." I nodded. "And your dick, well, I was a lady and didn't look but—"

"Bullshit." He laughed. "You were the opposite of good eye contact, more like, *oh look, a penis, let's stare at it and see if it grows.*"

"Well, I mean…water makes everything grow…right?" I countered.

"Not cold water." His smile was everything I craved, everything that made me forget that I was sad, a bit lost, and broken. His smile, just like tonight, was magic.

"Didn't seem to matter to me." I shrugged, wrapping my arms around his neck.

Our foreheads touched. "You hate me," he whispered.

"Hate is such a strong word," I said flippantly as our bodies rubbed together.

Another groan escaped his lips as the water lapped around our shoulders.

And then all chaos broke out as cousins came running toward the shore, stripping and jumping in.

Ash protectively shoved Annie behind him as she undressed, and then he carried her in.

Everyone else didn't give a shit.

Which I kind of loved.

"We heard yelling!" Serena laughed, splashing in. "And then we saw two naked-ass bodies."

"Guilty!" I called back. "He goes where I go. I get naked; he has no choice."

"Yes." King nodded his head. "Sounds like a good job if naked equals naked."

Tank barked out a laugh. "Yes, well, in her case, naked could also equal death so…"

"Risk-taker." King grinned knowingly. "I like your style."

Tank slowly released me as the ocean became crowded with my cousins, with my friends, family. I loved that they were there.

Including us.

Me.

But I was upset that whatever had just transpired between us was gone as Tank moved over to Ash and started shoving him under the water.

Annie watched with a wistful smile on her face. I swam over to her and laughed when Ash threatened to kill Tank only for Tank to shove him back down.

"Boys," I said.

"Men," she countered. "Or have you not noticed?"

"My cousin? Hell, no. I mean…he's pretty, everyone knows that, but I don't look at his pee-pee."

Annie giggled as water lapped around her pale skin. "I would hope not."

"Pretty sure it's illegal."

"Not in Kentucky." Maksim floated right on by on his back, dick in the air.

"EWWWW, MAKSIM!" I kicked his ass while Annie covered her face with one hand.

He just chuckled darkly and started singing row, row, row your boat, gently across the stream, life is but a penis dream…

"Something's wrong with him," I muttered.

I was about to shove him under the water when Izzy beat me to it. He gulped ocean water and then down he went.

She would kill him dead one day.

And he'd only have himself and his sad little penis song to blame.

"Hey!" a man yelled from the beach. Flashlights blinded us as more yelling ensued. "You can't swim after nine!"

"Lameeeeee!" Junior yelled. "Where's my gun?"

"I have a knife," Valerian said helpfully while Violet sighed as if she were disappointed. "What? I do. How else can I protect you?"

"Your fists," King said stoically. "GOD, STOP YELLING!" he roared toward shore. "It's like they don't understand that it's been weeks since any of us have killed someone."

Valerian snorted. "Speak for yourself."

"Showoff," Maksim muttered.

"Lots of blood?" Junior just had to ask while everyone leisurely made it toward the shore, ignoring the flashlights and yelling.

"Meh." Valerian shrugged. "Ask Ash. He's the one who went in for the final kill. Damn knife got lodged between a few ribs."

"My favorite knife," Ash swore. "Damn rats."

I grinned, loving it when they talked dirty because…hello, how else were we supposed to live this sort of life without having a nervous breakdown?

Normalize it.

Justify it.

I didn't say it was right. Or good.

It was, however, necessary.

"Get out before we call the cops!"

"I *am* the cops!" Tank yelled, earning laughter from everyone.

I mean, he wasn't wrong.

"Above the law, bitches." Ash fist-bumped Tank. "Badge up, bro. We've got your back."

"FBI, FBI!" Maksim chanted, followed by Junior and King.

I was surrounded by idiots.

"Get out!" the security guard yelled again, and another one joined him.

"Playing by the rules sucks," I said, mainly to myself. "Hey, does this resort still have that super cheesy club?"

"YES!" Junior pointed at me. "That's the enthusiasm we need tonight!"

We all rushed toward the shore in a naked blur, grabbing clothes, shoes, and running as Ash yelled out, "Twenty minutes!"

The security guards started reprimanding us, but all it took was one look from Tank as he literally pulled out his badge from his trouser pocket, and both security guards shrugged, nodded, and walked away.

Tank grinned and waved. "*Gracias.*"

I held my dress to the front of my body while Maksim moved next to me in a drunken blur.

"I'm too drunk…" Maksim stumbled in the sand. "But, hell yeah, twenty minutes… Wait, where are we going?"

"I got him." King laughed.

Valerian helped King get Maksim to his feet, and off they went while I semi-covered my body even more and shivered toward my hotel room.

"Hop on." Tank stopped next to me.

I looked down.

He sighed. "Yeah, I meant my back."

I shrugged. "But you understand my confusion, right?"

He gritted his teeth. "You're not helping, Tiny."

"That's one thing you are not…" I nodded. "Tiny."

"Get on before I get off from that pout," he barked.

My knees buckled a bit. "W-what?"

His eyes gleamed. "Ah, so she does have a weakness."

"And what's that?"

"Sex."

"Pleaseeeeee." I forced a laugh. "That's so far from the truth that—"

I was pinned next to the beach snack shack in a flash, heat vibrating from every part of Tank. "Oh?"

"We're going to be late."

"Mmmm…" He leaned in. "Scared?"

"No." I gave him a shove. "I just don't like getting poked in the face with dangerous weapons."

He smirked. "I'm not that tall."

"You were an inch deep in my belly button. It got weird. We can both wash our eyes with bleach later."

"Nice try, Tiny. Nice try." Tank started to turn around.

I used the opportunity to jump onto his back and hook my feet around his waist. "Question, if I orgasm by rubbing across your back, would that be weird?"

"Answer, if all it takes is my back to give you an orgasm—damn, girl, you've been doing it wrong this entire time."

I gasped and jumped off his back.

And then I was silent as we walked back toward our bungalow.

He didn't turn around when we got through the front door.

But I did hear the shower turn on.

I was too stunned by his playfulness.

By the fact that he wasn't backing down despite my attitude, my teasing.

It was like Tank had decided something.

I just wished I knew what.

Furthermore, I wished it didn't make me think that he might actually have feelings for me that went beyond annoyance.

I took a deep breath and went into my room.

First, a shower.

Second?

A dress that would get me answers. I was the mafia, I could crack—even Tank.

A smile formed across my lips.

He felt like teasing?

I'd be the biggest tease he'd ever seen.

Chapter Seven

Tank

She was killing me slowly with all that dancing, her arms up over her head as she swayed in the middle of the club dance floor. Cheesy techno lights pulsed in time with the beat of the music as the screen behind her showed a music video of some catchy song I'd never heard before.

Most of the girls danced with her.

Ash came and sat on the barstool next to me, whiskey in hand. "I've never been more stressed out than in this moment."

I snorted out a laugh. "Because you just now realized that every single one of your cousins is drop-dead gorgeous, along with your own family, and any guy watching this would probably rub one off on the spot?"

"Stop watching Annie," he barked with a smile.

"Please." I rolled my eyes. "I like living, and you know I was never…we never…fuck, stop making this awkward, you dick."

Valerian snorted out a laugh on the other side of me, only to have Ash peer around and go, "My sister. Slept with my sister. Get me another drink, bitch."

"I'm a boss. I don't have to—"

Ash growled.

"But sure, yeah, okay. Good idea." Valerian shot to his feet and walked over to the end of the bar where two bartenders were working.

"Never gonna let it go," I murmured.

"Never." Ash's eyes moved back to Annie as she drunkenly leaned against Serena and laughed. "Damn…be right back."

"Sure, you won't." I took another sip of my scotch and shook my head.

My drink was nearly gone. I should have had Valerian get me another, but I needed to stretch my legs anyway.

I was so damn tired.

Not just physically but emotionally. Mentally. I hated that I was keeping things from Kartini almost as much as I hated that it was nearly impossible not to want her despite her un-canny ability to make me want to pull my hair out and then strangle her.

My lips twitched as I walked up to the bar and set down my glass. I had to admit, it was pretty cool that besides the staff, we were the only guests there.

"What will you have?" The dark-haired woman turned around and grinned.

I glared, then looked down at her name tag. "Jennie?"

She shrugged. "Scotch? Arsenic?"

I gritted my teeth so hard I felt my jaw pop. "The hell are you doing here?"

"We all have our jobs, Tank." Giana batted her eyelashes. "And I'm here to finish mine."

"The hell you will." I jumped to my feet.

She just shrugged. "You have your orders. I have mine."

"Bullshit. They wouldn't send both of us."

"They would if they had their suspicions you would get cold feet…again. Besides, when you look out there, what do you see?"

I glanced over my shoulder.

"I see criminals. Enemies. The problem with you, Tank? You're so pathetically starved for love that you see friends."

"Touch any of them, and I'll slit your throat," I promised.

She poured me a drink and slid it toward me. "Touch me, and it will be the last time you do it, Tank."

"I'm calling Thompsons…"

She held out her cell and pointed the screen toward me. "No need. He's already asked for my ETA. Seems like you've been played, little man. One has to wonder why the FBI can't trust you anymore…then again,"—she looked around the room—"I guess you have your answer."

Confusion warred with rage. "He said it was my last job."

Nothing but the pulsing music, and then she grinned. "Exactly."

Son of a bitch!

They were playing me.

They *all* were.

But I trusted Thompsons. He was the closest thing I had to a father-figure, a stepdad in his own right. He'd found me. He'd helped me learn how to project my rage at the age of fifteen when I'd had nobody. Both of my parents were killed, and Thompsons knew that I would need to channel the anger I felt at losing them so young. I ended up becoming one of the youngest FBI recruits in the history of the Bureau. Then again, the government needed someone who was close in age to the bosses' kids—which meant I got to be the lucky volunteer.

I balled my fists and slammed the countertop so hard, my drink toppled over. Then, I stomped over to Valerian. "You drunk?"

"You okay?"

"No." I gulped. "I have to go talk to Sergio. You got eyes on Kartini?"

He shook his drink. "Club soda. One of us has to stay sober."

I sighed in relief. "You got any men watching?"

He just grinned. "Around seventeen associates are surrounding the club right now. I want them to have fun." He sighed. "They deserve it before they're forced to turn into…" His voice trailed off, and I knew he was referring to himself.

Nearly overnight, he'd gone from a manwhore college student to the youngest boss of the Petrov Family in history.

The weight of his family name was nearly heavier than Ash, Junior, and King's combined. Then again, the Russians weren't experiencing much peace at the moment, not with Valerian constantly having to prove himself over and over again.

I didn't even want to know how many people he'd killed in the past week.

I was sure it was daunting.

I slapped him on the shoulder. "I appreciate you."

He put his hand on my other shoulder and squeezed. "A word of advice?"

I nodded. He leaned forward and said in a low voice, "Trust no one."

"Not even you?"

"You'd be dead if you couldn't trust me," he said ruthlessly. "One day, you'll have to decide if you're willing to burn the world for one person or if your job means so much to you—your past—that you're willing to fuck up your future. That's your crown. That's your baggage. That's your cross to bear."

A chill ran down my spine as his eyes locked onto mine in warning.

"Thanks, Valerian."

"Anytime." He moved gracefully past me then, and my rage returned full-force as I thought of anyone hurting my family.

Mine.

I had no clue when they'd become mine, when I had started claiming them, when it had turned from a very lucrative job where I was backed into a corner with a gun pointed at my face to justifying crime, murder, and bloodshed.

And all in the name of family—*F*amily.

My thoughts were dark as I walked back down the club stairs and into the main pathway that led to the bungalows the adults and younger children were staying in.

Sergio had texted me his number for updates.

And while I hated interrupting his vacation, I had to know.

I knocked on number seven and didn't even flinch when two men appeared behind me as if I would make a run for it.

"Must you guys always sneak up on me?" I sighed. "It's not like you don't know me…"

Dom flashed me a sloppy grin. "I just like seeing you flinch."

Ax chuckled next to him.

"What? Are you guys gonna high-five now?"

"Should we?" Ax asked.

"I love a good high-five." Dom nodded.

I groaned and turned back just as the door jerked open. Sergio wore black silk pajama bottoms low on his hips, and his long, still-black hair fell across his massive shoulders. "This'd better be good."

"You look like Johnny Depp before the pirates." I laughed.

He growled.

My smile fell. "It was a compliment!"

He peered around me. "Are you two laughing?"

"Never." Ax choked on a laugh while Dom cleared his throat a million times.

Sergio sighed and then opened the door wider. "Come in." He jerked his head toward the two made men. "You two make another round."

"On it," Dom said quickly as the door shut behind me.

Sergio's bungalow was twice the size of the one I was staying in with Kartini. With floor-to-ceiling doors that opened out to the beach, white furniture, a roaring fireplace near a flat-screen TV, and a spiraled wooden staircase that I was sure led to the several bedrooms.

"The wife sleeping?"

His glare said that they'd been doing something other than sleeping and that I'd interrupted.

I winced. "Sorry, bad timing."

"When is it ever good timing to have an FBI agent in your bungalow?" He walked over to the bar. "Wine?"

"No. I'll be quick."

"You may need it."

"Then I want whiskey."

His chuckle was dark as his muscles moved and stretched. The man may be in his fifties, but he was jacked.

Tattoos covered his chest, swirling down his massive arms as he held out a glass with one ice cube and two shots poured into it. "Speak."

"How long?"

"Pardon?" He sat in the leather chair across from me. "You'll have to be more specific. I can't read minds."

"How long, Sergio?" I repeated. "Have you known?"

His expression was impassive, and then he said, "Why else would I have you guard her?"

I shook my head. "You knew they planned to kidnap her? And take her out by any means necessary to get you guys to talk?"

He leaned back in his chair. "Serena's a fighter, she would have probably beheaded one of them and laughed. Izzy's not far behind. The rest of the girls are younger—they wouldn't dare. But Kartini? Perfect little Kartini...she's the perfect target, don't you think? Related to basically every boss, Nixon's niece, my daughter, Chase's niece. Tex's niece by marriage...Dante's cousin..."

I squeezed my eyes shut. "I couldn't do it."

"Of course, you couldn't. I knew they would one day ask it of you—that they wouldn't be happy with you infiltrating the Families for the sake of feeding them information. Knew they'd get greedy—and my daughter nearly died because of it."

I froze. "I didn't touch her."

"You didn't..." He nodded. "You also failed to protect her."

I groaned and tipped back my drink. "Who did?"

"That's what I'd like to know. Were they FBI? Were they just in the right place at the right time? Did they have orders like you? Was it just horribly executed and not related? The trail begins and stops at the FBI. My only question is this…what do they have to gain by hurting my daughter, Tank?"

I knew the answer.

I knew it before it was even asked for me to kidnap her, bloody her up, make it look bad—and do it all at this wedding for all to see.

I swallowed the dryness in my throat. "War."

"Ah." Sergio lifted his glass into the air. "Nothing the FBI loves more than when the Families are fighting amongst themselves…"

"Shit." I ran my hands through my hair, mussing it. "So that's why I'm here watching her now? And you knew the FBI would send in agents, didn't you?"

"I assumed so, yes. They no longer trust you. You're straddling a line that no longer allows you to touch both sides safely. One day, you'll have to choose, and that day I'm afraid is coming sooner rather than later… Protect her, Tank—with your life. And then we talk."

"And if it's my life that's taken in order to keep her safe?"

He was quiet, then he whispered, "Then I'll give you a king's burial and pray for your soul."

"Thought so." I stood. "Sergio?"

He looked up.

"Did she have anything to do with the killings that day? At the beach?"

"That…" His eyes were wild. "Is not my story to tell. I trust that the day Kartini feels she can talk to you about it is the day you'll have to make your choice, Tank."

That's what I was worried about.

"Thanks for the drink." I left my glass and showed myself out. My mood was dark as I traced my steps back to the club.

The music was too loud.

The night too long.

Kartini danced around Annie now, swaying her hips left and right.

And I snapped.

Something fucking snapped as I stomped toward the dance floor, picked her up, and threw her over my shoulder.

Most of the guys just gave me knowing grins.

All but Valerian, who narrowed his eyes as if to warn me.

"Put me down!" Tiny batted her fists against my back as I carried her down the stairs toward our bungalow. "Tank, I'm serious! This is ridiculous."

I slapped her on the ass and then groaned. "What the hell did I say about underwear?"

"Forgot it all at home." She burst out laughing as I gave her body another shake. "Hey!"

"Bedtime," I rasped.

"What, I have a curfew now? God, you're so depressingly olddddddd." She kicked her feet as her heels nearly fell to the ground. "Hey, let's go get a tattoo."

"And that's why you're going to bed."

"Killjoy."

"Yes, but you're alive. So, you're welcome."

"I'm finnneeee!" She sighed. "Nobody's tried anything since that threat I didn't even know about…a year ago." She stilled.

"Something to confess?"

"I think about you when I shower?"

I tripped on my next step. "Not funny."

"What makes you think I'm lying? Maybe I should buy a vibrator and name it Tank just to mess with you at night, screaming your name. I bet that would kill you, your name falling from my lips only to know it's a robot giving me pleas—"

I slapped her ass so hard my hand stung.

"OW!" She wiggled. "That's gonna leave a mark."

"Good." I slid the keycard and pushed the door open with my foot, then stomped into the master bedroom, tossing her onto the bed.

She bounced up, down, back up, and then glared. Her blue hair stuck to her lip gloss as she shoved it out of the way, and then she crossed her arms, her breasts nearly spilling out of whatever the hell that tiny scrap of black material was.

The plunging neckline went nearly to her belly button, and she was having trouble covering her thighs.

"Bedtime," I growled.

She leaned back on her hands and crossed her legs. "You joining me, Tank?"

"Yes." I peeled my shirt over my head and tossed it to the floor. "As a matter of fact, I am."

Her expression went from confident to pale, then back again. "W-what?"

"You're not…scared, are you, Tiny?"

She scowled. "Never. I just don't want to catch any STDs from your dick. If it touches me, I'm cutting it off with a blunt knife!"

"Sounds exciting. Tell me more." I yawned. "Now, do I need to help you get your pajamas on, or can we sleep? You're exhausting."

"Don't you mean you're exhausted?"

"Nope, I said it right." I flashed a smile. "Well?"

She stood and lifted her chin, then walked over to where I'd thrown my shirt and pulled it over her head. It fell to her knees, and then she very slowly pulled down the straps of her dress and shimmied out of it until it dropped to the floor.

I could see her nipples through my white shirt.

"Ready," she announced.

"You don't believe in pajamas?" I shifted on my feet.

She took a step toward me and patted me on the stomach. "I sleep in the nude…you're welcome."

I couldn't contain the groan that left my lips just like she seemed unable to contain the blush that stained her cheeks.

I shoved down my jeans and crawled into bed in nothing but my black boxer briefs, and waited as a dull roar pulsed in my ears.

She was in the bathroom.

Minutes later, the lights turned off, and she crawled into bed beside me.

In my shirt.

A mere foot from my arms.

My hands twitched.

She sighed.

I sighed.

And I hated that every part of me that was male came alive—burned to reach across that mattress and pull her against me.

My life or hers.

That was what I'd been cryptically told by all sides tonight.

Me.

Or this small, terrifying woman sleeping next to me with her veiled threats, blue hair, constant mockery, and gorgeous blue eyes.

I always wondered what it was like when people knew they were going to die. Was it sad? Depressing as hell? Or did it make them come alive?

Because I felt alive.

In that moment.

I wanted to touch, lick, experience. Please.

Because there was a great possibility that when she boarded the plane back home, a certain FBI agent would no longer be with her.

Me.

Her.

I sighed. "You," I whispered. "Every time."

Chapter Eight

Kartini

"You," he whispered. "Every time."

I froze.

My eyes had been closed.

But he had to know I wasn't asleep yet. How could I possibly be asleep with my body humming the way it was? He was so close.

After wanting him from afar.

And now…he was in my bed.

I sobered immediately when he shifted.

Held my breath when the mattress dipped.

And then a strong arm jerked me against a warm body.

I opened my mouth to say something snarky when Tank whispered in my ear, his breath hot, his tongue touching skin. "For once…don't."

But, of course, I did. "Are you protecting me or holding me, Tank?"

He nuzzled my hair a bit with his nose. My lips parted on a little gasp of surprise as he whispered, "A little bit of both."

I gulped. "You, um…brought your gun to bed."

A dark chuckle and then. "No."

Holy shit.

Holy. Shit.

Mouth dry, I just lay there with his giant arm pinned across my body, his breath in my hair, and his very aroused body pressed up against me.

I could literally feel every pulsing heartbeat of that giant non-gun in his pants.

And it seemed the more I felt, the more I wanted to feel.

I wiggled a bit.

He bit back a curse. "Bad idea."

"Or best idea I've ever had, and we can blame it on intoxication."

"Sober."

I sighed. "Same."

He let out a little growl. "Good to know that's the only way you'd screw me, Tiny." He pulled me tighter against him. "Now, stop wiggling and sleep."

"Fine."

"Good."

"One more thing—"

"If you say one more word, I'm gagging you, and it won't be the fun type of gag where you have a safe word."

I perked up. "Should we make a safe word just in case?"

He cursed.

"Sea turtle." I decided with a cheerful sigh. "They're innocent enough and—"

His hand moved up and cupped over my mouth.

I kind of liked it.

In a weird way.

How the hell did his hand smell so good, anyway?

Was that lotion?

Tank?

Or just…man?

I shivered.

"Felt that," he hissed.

"It was involuntary," I snapped.

His chuckle made me want to stab him more than kiss him. So arrogant. How rude! "You know, you don't need to hold me."

Not that I could get away if I wanted to, but I wasn't about to admit defeat to the giant behind me.

If anything, he pulled me tighter against him, as if he were afraid to let me go. It was nice. Nice being wanted. Held. It had been…a while since anyone had simply held me or even wanted to.

I was too crass.

Too loud.

Too perfect one day, only to be too immature and crazy the next.

I never seemed to fit.

But I fit here.

In his arms.

I fit very well with his chin on my head, his hands on my skin, my heart beating out of my chest as his breathing slowed—seductively.

"I do, though." His voice sounded heavier, carrying a rasp of exhaustion that I felt deep in my bones. "Need to hold you."

It was on the tip of my tongue to ask him why.

But then something happened.

I actually relaxed.

His deep breathing told me that he'd done the same, though he still had me pinned against him like I was his favorite bear to sleep with. But I was oddly okay with it in that moment as I was lulled into a deep sleep.

And this time…

I didn't wake up screaming like I had after my first kill.

This time, I slept.

When my heavy eyes blinked open, a few hours had passed, and the warmth I'd felt from Tank's body was gone, leaving me shivering as I pulled the covers up over my body and sat up, looking around the room.

The shower was on.

I checked my phone.

Three a.m.? Really?

Rat bastard needs to shower at three a.m.?

With a groan, I chucked a pillow onto the floor and padded my way into the en suite bathroom.

Steam billowed outside of the walk-in shower. I mean, seriously, the hell was he doing?

I opened my mouth to yell something close to that when he walked around the shower wall, fully erect and nearly slipped back against the tile. "What are you doing?"

"It's nighttime! What do you think I was doing? I was sleeping!" I kept my eyes on his face.

I should have been given an award for that.

He was just so male.

"I couldn't sleep so I went for a quick perimeter run, then *still* couldn't sleep so did some pushups and—wait, why am I explaining myself to you again?"

"Soooo, my bodyguard left me?" My right eyebrow arched.

"Miss me?" He winked. "And don't worry, your bodyguard never left the premises, and I did the pushups inside the living room."

"How many?" I just had to ask.

"Three hundred." He sighed. "Now, can I dry off?"

"Who got your back?"

"Pardon?"

"In the shower." I lifted my chin. "Who got your back?"

"Is this a trick question?"

"Does it feel like it?"

He groaned. "Well, at least now I'm tired. Next time, I'm just going to wake you up and get a good verbal spar on. I'll be snoring in seconds."

"Because I'm boring?" I put my hands on my hips.

He rolled his eyes. "No, because you're exhausting."

"Oh"

"Yeah." He must have seen the frustration on my face because rather than grab a towel, he walked back into the shower, turned it on, and said, "You coming, or not?"

He'd called my bluff.

And now I had to wash his back.

His very buff back.

Me and my big, fat mouth.

I liked goading him.

He made me feel—more normal that way.

So, with an irritated sigh meant for myself, I pulled his t-shirt over my head, then very slowly walked around the corner and into the shower.

Both showerheads were on.

Steam billowed everywhere again.

Without turning around, Tank handed me a washcloth, and I went to work, my eyes traveling down his tanned muscular back like a woman starved.

It wasn't like I'd never had sex.

Just last year, I'd decided to get it over with and had been so disappointed that I literally lay there and went, "That was it?"

It was just a random guy from Eagle Elite. We were at a party, and I pulled him into a room and started making out with him. I'd wanted it over with. I'd wanted to feel—to feel something other than that deep, etched sadness.

And he had done nothing to make me feel better.

If anything, I was so disappointed when it hurt and then when he pumped his hips a magical three times—only to spill into me with a roar that definitely wasn't deserved—I mean, he didn't even do any work!

My body was still in pain.

I was sticky.

And I kind of wanted to pull my knife on him.

Okay, not kind of.

We never spoke again after that, and though I'd made out with a few guys since then out of sheer boredom, nobody had ever made me feel how Tank did—from just washing his stupid old-man back.

Ugh.

I wanted to slap the rag against his skin.

Instead, I moved my hand in a circular motion as if I were super confident and could stay there all night long.

"Done," I announced.

"Your turn." He turned around, his green eyes flashing as he took the rag from my hand and then made a turning motion with his hand.

Slowly, I did just that and let out a little gasp when he moved a tendril of hair, tucking it into my messy bun as he continued washing, moving the washcloth up and down my back, then side to side.

Chills erupted down my arms despite the hot water. When I thought he would say something snarky or just drop the washcloth, his hand moved again, the cloth swiftly passing from my lower back to the front of my hips, then up across my belly button and beneath my breasts as he slowly massaged and seduced.

A shudder ran through my body like an electric current. How was he doing this with a stupid washcloth?

How was I responding so fervently to a small touch like this?

"Last year…" Tank moved closer until his wet chest pressed against my back, his thick length pulsing against my lower back and butt. "I almost kissed you last year."

"What stopped you?" I asked.

"It was either kiss or kill. And perhaps the sickest part about this entire dilemma is that I think it would have been easier to kill you than to kiss you and have you walk away or reject me."

I grabbed his wrist, the washcloth frozen by my breasts. "And now? Now, what do you want?"

My pulse thudded in my ears as I waited.

He was my bodyguard.

But my brain never forgot about the badge he carried around.

And about what that meant with a last name like mine.

"Kiss." He let out a rough exhale. "Definitely kiss."

He flipped me around in his arms and lifted me against the tile wall, his mouth crashing against mine as I tried to match him kiss for kiss, tongue for tongue, his hips pressed into me, making it impossible not to feel the throbbing heat of him.

With a grunt, he pulled away, his green eyes gleaming with lust. "Is the safe word still Sea turtle?" He winked. "Just checking."

My jaw hung a bit before I spoke. "Did you really just kiss me and make a joke like my dad wouldn't murder you if he found out?"

"I kissed you, but you seduced me. Big difference."

"I did not!" I put my hands on my hips. "I've never even—"

His mouth covered mine again, and with a whimper, I dug my hands into his hair, tugging at his golden-brown locks, shamelessly rubbing my body against his.

He broke away, panting. "Did, too. Every day for the last year, you've been tempting me to either strangle you or turn you over onto my knee and spank the hell out of you for being so argumentative...so, really, this is all your fault. I'm sure he'll see it my way."

"It was just one kiss," I argued.

"Two." And then he lowered his mouth again, a gorgeous smirk forming across his lips. "Three." Another kiss. "Four." He backed away.

With a growl, I pulled his head back. "What? Can't count past four?"

He grinned against my mouth, then slowly lowered me to my feet.

"I really start to struggle when I get past five, yes." Tank turned off the water and turned to walk away.

"Wait!" I started to shiver. "That's it? You just confess you had a choice to kill or kiss me, then kiss me, then count way too high for your tiny brain, and now you're just leaving me naked in a shower, dripping wet?"

"Dripping wet?" His eyebrows shot up as he checked me out slowly. "No, you're not. But you will be."

"You—you!"

His answer was to toss a towel at my face.

With a growl, I dried off then wrapped it around myself as I marched into the bedroom to give him a piece of my mind—only to have him hold a finger up to his lips for me to be quiet.

I nodded jerkily and stayed put as he slowly reached for the nightstand and pulled out a gun I didn't even realize he'd been keeping there.

It was eerily quiet.

And then, a small creak sounded.

Followed by another.

For a man so large, he moved with the grace of a predator. Someone in all black suddenly flashed through the living room.

Tank dove after the person.

They both went crashing into the coffee table, scrambling onto the floor as Tank pinned him, punching him in the face repeatedly until blood caked his fingertips. The person looked as if they weren't breathing.

"Is he dead?" I whispered.

Tank's answer was to growl, get off the guy, then kick him as if he were testing to see if he was still breathing. "Grab my cell."

I didn't realize I was shaking until I grabbed his phone from his side of the bed and handed it to him.

He dialed a number, held it to his ear, and spoke in low tones. "Yeah, just one…no." He looked back at me. "She's safe. Uh-huh, cleanup won't take long. No, she's fine. I said she's fine. Allow me to do my job. Thank you…" He hung up. "Your dad says he loves you and that if I touch you, I'll die a horrible death. He did mention something about fire, gasoline, and chickens—honestly, the chickens freak me out the most."

I just stared. "How are you even talking so casually? This guy just got the shit beat out of him, and he was spying on me—on us. What if he would have come into the bathroom?"

Tank shrugged. "Then I would have killed him, and we wouldn't have broken the coffee table."

I gulped. "Is this why Dad has you guarding me?"

"You tell me." Tank's eyes flashed. "Because a year ago at Valerian's wedding, you were supposed to be kidnapped. It was going to be FBI-led. They wanted division between the Petrov Family and the rest of the Italians again. That's all I was told. And the only thing that makes sense is that united, you're too strong, and the FBI loses its foothold—the minute I make a choice they already knew I was going to make."

All the breath I'd been holding left my chest as I locked eyes with him. I wondered in that moment if I would lose him.

Not just his anger.

His rage.

But also his teasing.

The way he held me.

The way he protected me, even when he wanted to do more than that.

And the way he touched me.

Was I damning myself?

And, at the end of the day, could I truly trust this man standing in front of me, asking to take the leap into his arms when I knew that the ending could end up in handcuffs or worse—death?

But my dad…he trusted him.

I loved my dad.

I would die for him.

So, if he said that Tank was my bodyguard, then I could trust him with my life.

Therefore, I opened my mouth and said, "You didn't save me…" And burst into tears.

Chapter Nine

Tank

I didn't know what to do.

But the last thing I needed was her bawling in front of the crime scene—or having whoever they sent seeing her upset and reporting back to Sergio.

So, I promptly scooped her into my arms, opened the sliding glass door, and walked out onto the beach until I found an empty Cabana with its sides pulled tight around it.

She was still sniffling when I sat down on one of the lounge chairs with her still on my lap, her head resting against my chest as if it belonged there.

I'd made the right choice.

I knew that now.

I just needed a reality check of what that meant, what it could mean if this went wrong. If the Family that I chose either double-crossed me—or chose not to protect me.

God, it hurt.

That space where my heart beat against my rib cage, that space where my heart beat for her over and over again.

Could I even regret such a thing?

No.

Not even a little bit.

"What happened...?" I whispered. "That day."

Kartini stilled, and then she pulled away from me just enough to look at her hands—as if they were stained with blood.

"You weren't there."

"But I was…" I corrected. "I was there when Ash was being an ass per usual. I was there when we went to the bar. And I was there when you ran off because you didn't want them to see your tears."

She shuddered against me, still refusing to lift her head so I could see the sweetness of her blue eyes.

"There were two men." She sighed. "They hit on me earlier that night. I turned them down because, obviously, I couldn't look like I was with someone else when all my energy was spent on trapping you."

I froze. "I'm sorry, what?"

"I may have"—she twisted her hands in her lap—"had a small, non-important crush on you."

"What?"

"Are you really going to make me repeat the humiliation, Tank?"

"Having a crush on me's humiliating?"

"Okay, that came out wrong. Tuck your tender dick away and just listen, okay? Otherwise, I won't be able to get this out." She sighed.

"My dick isn't tender."

Another sigh. "I'm aware. I can feel it."

Weirdly enough, I felt my cheeks heat right along with the rest of my body.

Crush.

She'd had a crush?

Had as in past tense.

So, what did she have now? An aversion? Hatred?

Shit.

She really should not have told me that.

She flirted with anyone and everyone. And while, yes, the plan was to get answers from her, I realized I was compelled to flirt right back. To see how far I could push her, to see how much I could touch her, to see how much I could have her.

"So, what happened?" I finally asked with extreme strength that I somehow gathered from whatever well of it I had left after hearing that news. "You can trust me."

Finally, she looked up into my eyes. "I ran away like the little girl you said I was. I cried, like the child you saw me as." My heart clenched. "And then, in less than seven minutes, I went from little girl to woman. I went from innocent to guilty. I went from Heaven to Hell, and I've been there ever since."

Tears slid down her face in rapid succession.

I wiped them from her cheeks. "Why?"

"He said he was going to kill me." Her voice was hoarse. "He-he touched me."

My fingers clenched into fists.

"And he kept trying to touch me." She lowered her head. "He ripped my dress." All I saw was murder. "He wasn't just going to kidnap me. He wanted to screw me before or after I was dead, didn't seem to matter to him. He was using me as an example maybe? I never figured out who he was connected to, and neither could my dad. It was maybe a hazard of being in the mafia, a one-time thing, you know? All I know is that one minute he was trying to kill me, and the next, my knife was in his stomach, and I was pushing. He was bleeding. And then all my training came back full-force. I was at his back, choking him, we fell back against the rocks on the cliffs."

Slowly, she turned in my arms. "You never asked about the small scars on my back…they're from the rocks."

"I don't notice scars," I said honestly, because I hadn't. "I just notice your beauty, Tiny."

She wiped under her eyes. "Thanks."

"So, he died?" My stomach clenched.

"I killed him," she admitted. "To save myself. And I'd do it again."

I was quiet for a few heartbeats as the ocean waves crashed against the shore. I pulled her against my chest and kissed the top of her head. "You did well."

"Am I in trouble?"

"That depends…"

"On?"

"Did that fucker suffer?" Rage burned behind my eyes.

She hiccupped out a sob and then a laugh. "I hope so."

"Good." I kissed her head again. "Did he ever tell you his name?"

"He said his name was Jenner, that's all I know. It wasn't in any databases. Trust me, my dad looked them up."

It wouldn't be in any databases.

It was his code name.

The name of a spy.

My stomach rolled. "What did he look like?"

"Tall, blond, handsome." She shuddered. "A monster."

Jenner had been on my team.

The same one Giana and I had partnered on.

The team I'd told to stand down that day, even though Giana saw an opportunity. And they should have. I thought they had. And then Jenner went missing, and I assumed that he'd gotten drunk and wandered off.

Drowned.

Or got his ass killed by being in the wrong place at the wrong time at a mafia wedding.

I was close.

Not close enough.

The very bureau I had trusted—worked for—had carried out a hit on the precious woman sitting in my arms, crying. Forced to make her first kill.

Forced her to become made, when all she'd wanted was to flirt with me and dance with her dad.

Agony ripped through me.

I wanted to scream.

I wanted to burn the entire world down.

And now I knew why Sergio had put me in this position.

He wanted me to see it firsthand.

He didn't want to tell me that we were all villains because who would you believe? The one with the badge, or the one with the gun pointed at her head?

"Do you know what happened after?" I asked quietly. Already, I was afraid of what she would say.

"Dad said he would deal with it. But it was my kill. Mine. It was my life. Not his. So, I chopped off Jenner's head and made a choice—to send a warning to everyone who could possibly be involved. His head was delivered to the FBI in a cake box. And since I had no way of knowing if they had any involvement, I covered my bases and sent his hand to Valerian—after all, it was at their wedding. And then I sent a foot to the Carola Cartel. And since he had one foot left, I decided that he could still walk in Hell. So, I burned it. Maksim helped me, and my dad watched in horror, knowing I'd never be the same. I tried washing the blood from my hands, but it's still there. I still see it." She choked on a sob. "It won't come off. God, it won't come off." She shook in my arms.

I quickly turned her on my lap so her body straddled mine on the chair. She'd never been more vulnerable—or more beautiful.

"You did good, Kartini. So damn good."

Her eyes narrowed in confusion. "You shouldn't praise me for killing."

"I'm not praising you for killing." I tucked pieces of her blue hair behind her ears. "I'm praising you for surviving."

Her blue eyes flashed, scanning mine. I didn't know what happened next, but my hands tightened on her curvy waist as if my body, my fingers, knew how desperately I needed to keep her close.

Forever.

To protect her.

Fight beside her.

Mark her.

"Tank…" She licked her lips.

I caught her tongue with my mouth, licking the seam of her lips and pulling her hard against me as her tears fell across my cheeks and rolled down my face, colliding with our mouths.

It was a moment I would never forget.

Kissing her tears away.

Drinking in her pain.

"Never again," I said between long, languid kisses. "You'll never be alone again."

"What are you saying?" Her bottom lip was swollen from my mouth, from sucking on it, from holding it where I wanted it, pinning it with my teeth, pinching it, only to suck it again.

"I'm not a knight in shining armor. I'm more villain, who's always pretended to be the hero," I admitted. "But now, I know who I am. Because of you."

"And who's that?"

"Yours…" I said. "A half-De Lange."

She gasped.

"A made man." Her eyes filled with more tears.

"Loyal to the Five Families."

"And the FBI?" she asked.

I nipped at her mouth and whispered, "Let it fucking burn."

Chapter Ten

Kartini

He didn't judge me.

Instead, he loved me. Devoured my pain with his mouth.

De Lange.

We all knew, but for him to openly admit it—it was like watching a healing take place across his face as he finally confessed his truth.

And another De Lange orphan had joined the fold.

Had joined us.

Repenting for the sins of the father.

Earning my respect and that of the Five Families. I couldn't be prouder or happier or more interested in ripping his clothes off.

I clawed at his naked chest, forgetting that he'd basically carried me out there in nothing but a towel wrapped around his waist, one wrapped around my body.

With a curse, he pulled mine loose.

I was completely bare to him—naked, needy.

His hands cupped my breasts as he flipped me onto my back. I took his towel with me.

Both of us were naked, grinding against each other as the waves crashed on the shore. And rather than wanting to get it over with, I wanted this moment to last forever.

He was mine.

He would always be mine.

His mouth pressed against my neck as he moved down to my belly button, his eyes meeting mine with wicked promises and relentless pursuit. "Still have a crush?"

My body responded as I spread my thighs. "What do you think?"

"I think I would be starving for you even if I'd never met you." He lowered his head. "And I'm not fighting it anymore."

"Don't."

"I told you, you'd be wet before the end of the night." His laugh was dark as his eyes flashed, and then his mouth clamped down on me, his tongue darting out to find every sensitive inch that screamed for his attention.

My head rolled back and hit the soft pad of the chair as he tasted me, filling me with nothing but his tongue but making it feel like it was more than that—more than anything I'd ever had in my life.

"Don't stop," I begged. I never begged. This was the Tank effect.

He did stop, though, just enough to lift his cocky head, just enough to dig his fingertips into my thighs, just enough to give me a knowing smirk, his mouth glistening. "Did you just beg?"

"Let it go, Tank."

His eyes were fierce, nearly feral. "Do it again."

I started to move, to close my legs.

"Oh no, you don't." He held them open, his hands strong, his golden muscles taut. He was like this massive god, like Poseidon capturing a willing human on the beach and feasting. "I want to experience you saying it. I wanna hear it. I want you, Kartini Abandonato, to beg me."

"For what?" My body trembled, totally giving me away as the warmth of the night air blew across my naked skin.

"Me," he finally said. "I want you to beg for me. For my mouth wherever you want it, however long you need it. For my cock—" He slowly crawled up my body, easily covering me as he held himself over me and whispered against my mouth so I could taste myself on his lips. "Beg."

"You think you can fight me and win?" I taunted.

He rolled a nipple between his fingertips then lowered his head and sucked, sending shockwaves through my system. "You think you wanna rephrase that question, princess?"

"Damn it!" I bucked against him. "Why can't you be like normal guys? Get me off, give me an orgasm, and be happy about it!"

"Because"—his green eyes flashed—"I'll never be happy until I have complete surrender. I'll never be happy with pieces of you. I crave the entire thing."

Tears burned the backs of my eyes. "You mean it?"

"I swear it." His forehead touched mine.

I clawed at him, needing him to be closer as I pulled his head down to mine, our mouths colliding in an explosion of chaos as I tugged at his hair. My legs wrapped around his body, not even able to go halfway as I tried to get closer and failed.

"Please," I begged. "Please, Tank…I need you. I needed you then. I need you now."

He groaned, reaching between us, feeling how slick I was between my thighs, ready for him. "You're perfect."

I moved his hand away and gripped his cock, guiding it toward my entrance. "This, this is what I need."

"We don't have a condom." His chest heaved as if he were having trouble breathing and hated himself at the same time for saying something in that moment.

I just grinned. "Birth control. You think any of our dads would let us out of their sight without it?"

"Tiny…" His lips tugged again at mine, nipped, then kissed, healed. "Let's never discuss your dad or anyone else's again mid-sex, okay?"

I laughed against his mouth. "Good talk."

"And now…" He thrust inside me with one smooth movement. "No more talking."

I groaned as he started to move, then pounded at his back when he stopped, only to hear his wicked chuckle each time I got upset.

I'd never felt anything better than being full of him, then feeling his weight against me, him inside me. This was bliss. This was what I'd been missing, like I'd been walking around half of a person for a year.

All I'd needed was for this irritatingly attractive man to make me realize that I'd always been whole.

"Harder."

"If I go any harder and faster, this is going to be over really quick." He laughed and then groaned as I clawed at his back more. "Fuck."

"Yes, that. I want that." I laughed against his mouth. "Tank, Tank, I think—I don't know—"

"You're so close."

I felt myself tightening, spiraling out of control as I clung to his sweaty skin.

The sound of our bodies moving together, slapping…something about it, combined with the sound of the ocean waves, made me lose it.

Two thrusts later, Tank followed suit.

Panting, we looked at each other, our eyes locking.

A throat cleared.

"Um, yes. Hi, this is Maksim. You know, your cousin who did not, for the record, pull the cabana sheet back and take a peek. Um, the bosses require your uh, presence—"

"Shut up, man, you're making it worse!" King hissed. "Yo, hey, haha so…funny story, we saw you guys come down here, waited like ten minutes, then thought maybe you er, fell asleep." He coughed. "And, surprise, you were—"

"Not." Maksim finished. "I mean, at least that's not how I sleep, but to each his own, man. To each his own."

"No. Way." I covered my face with my hands.

"Good job, Tank!" King felt the need to say. "Ouch, what? At least, she got where…you know what? You're right, we won't talk about this."

"Never happened!" Maksim agreed. "We uh, brought clothes."

Tank squeezed his eyes shut. "You've got to be shitting me."

I fell back against the chair and blew out a breath. "Well, I guess at least they brought us clothes."

Tank burst out laughing, and then I joined him as we lay there a hot mess—naked and sweaty.

He leaned down and pressed another kiss to my mouth. "We'll see the bosses, and then I'm locking you in the master suite for the rest of the night."

I nodded. "Only if you promise to be naked."

"I'll even let you tie me to the bed. I know how your brain works. Just don't leave me there with an erection, 'kay?"

"Haha, no promises. Better keep me happy." I trailed a finger down his chest.

He grabbed my hand and kissed it.

"Guyssssss." Maksim's voice came again. "Good for you for blowing off some steam, but they said ten minutes, and it's been way longer. And you still have to somehow get that sex smell off of you, which, honestly, it's even out here. So maybe…walk faster, Tank, so Sergio doesn't break your legs for screwing his daughter?"

"Good point." Tank pulled away from me and then went to the opening of the cabana to poke his head out. "Clothes?"

Maksim said something I couldn't hear.

Then there was laughter.

Tank kicked at someone.

And then he closed the cabana again.

"Everything okay?" I leaned back on my elbows and watched him approach.

He swore and dropped my sarong and flip-flops onto the other chair. "No. You're naked, and now you have to put on clothes... Oh, and Maksim's a jackass."

"Heard that!" Maksim called.

"You really are, though," King agreed, loudly.

I threw my head back and laughed. "You're no saint either, King!"

"Love you, Tiny!"

"Love you, too!"

We hurried and got dressed, discarded the er...towels we'd used to wipe each other down, and quickly started walking with Maksim and King.

It was quiet.

Which was rare with those two.

"I can't keep it in," Maksim blurted. "I tried extremely hard, but I just can't do it, it may kill me." He turned his perfect fallen-angel face toward me and smirked. "Tank and Tiny...How did he even—?"

Tank lunged for him.

But Maksim was fast.

Probably because he had a mouth on him and had to learn how to run away so he didn't have to fight. Even though he could probably take on Tank, Tank was still bigger.

King busted up laughing. "He only said what everyone's going to be thinking."

I stumbled. "Everyone?"

"Please." Maksim jogged back. "It's all over your faces." He snorted. "Especially this guy's." He pointed to Tank. "His face literally says, *Just got laid, five stars, one hundred percent recommend!*"

"I'm killing you," Tank said in a low voice.

"Many have tried." Maksim just grinned. "All have failed. I'm too pretty."

King sighed. "Pretty doesn't keep you alive."

"And yet, it does." Maksim shrugged. "One of the world's great mysteries, I suppose. Oh, and"—he snapped his fingers—"future boss of the Sinacore Family. No big…"

Tank just laughed. "If you make it that long."

"Hey, hey." Maksim slapped him on the back. "I was just curious. Besides, it's not like anyone can keep a secret around here when people are having sex, need I refresh your young minds about the DoorDash incident with Annie and Ash outside, pants down at his ankles? I'm still traumatized, and I'm all for outside sexcapades."

King shuddered. "Some things, I should never have to see. One being my cousin's mouth on"—he gulped—"…never mind. I'm still not okay."

"It will get better." Maksim wrapped an arm around him. "These things take time."

"It was so cold that night." King put his head on Maksim's shoulder. "And the lights—"

"There, there." Maksim gave him a slight hug and then shoved him.

And I realized, I hadn't stopped smiling.

Tank grabbed my hand.

And I knew as we approached the large structure housing Tex, my uncle and Godfather of the Families, that it would be okay.

I had Tank.

And neither of us were letting go.

Chapter Eleven

Tank

I don't know what I expected.

But all the bosses lined up in the living room of the hut in the dark with candles lit all around them was not one of those things.

Sergio took one look at me holding Kartini's hand and straight-up growled like a fucking animal.

Nixon put his hand on his shoulder and pulled him back.

Tex—the terrifying Capo—grinned like a fool.

Valerian stood next to him, arms folded, eyes lasered in on me as if telling me it was time.

And it was.

Every boss was present.

Dante Alfero, Tex Campisi, Phoenix Nicolasi, Andrei Sinacore, Valerian Petrov, Nixon Abandonato—and underbosses Chase Abandonato, Ash's dad, and next to him, still glaring...

Sergio.

I had no clue if I was about to become a fucking sacrifice to some mafia god or if they were about ready to offer me what Valerian had known I wanted.

I'd already been made, so I wasn't sure what the hell this was, but it must have been important because Kartini squeezed my hand extra-hard, and I could tell just by the look on her face how important this really was.

Only the older kids were there.

Ash, King, Maksim, Junior, Izzy, Serena, Annie, and Violet all stood off to the side, and then slowly Ash moved forward.

I frowned as Ash, one of my best friends despite the fact that this last year we'd nearly killed each other, moved directly in front of me.

His blue eyes nearly glowed, his whiskey-colored hair fell in a mess over his forehead, and I was reminded yet again how regal he looked when he was being serious and not pissed.

He looked me straight in the eyes then held a card up between us. "Do you know what this is?"

It was a white piece of paper. Written on it...in what looked like blood, was a name. St. Christopher.

I gulped. "The name of a Saint?"

Ash nodded. "The name of yours. St. Christopher is believed to be a protector. From hurricanes, floods, sickness, and danger. The bosses voted and gave me two options for your ceremony. Ever since we met you two years ago, you've protected us. Whether from the outside FBI threat, or the threat from within the Family." My heart pounded in my chest. I felt like I couldn't breathe. "This is your marker. This will always be your marker from this day forward, Tank De Lange." He said my real name. My real bloodline. The one I'd originally hidden from everyone.

The bosses didn't even flinch.

Not even Chase, the man who'd killed so many of my family that it was downright terrifying.

They knew I had De Lange blood somewhere down the line.

"Your grandmother was a De Lange," Ash said with a smile. "We finally found some records the FBI had on lockdown. You can thank Sergio for that hack."

Could I, though? Did I even want to go down that road? Know what my family had done in the name of the De Lange bloodline? No. Because I had a new Family now—the ones standing in front of me.

I lifted my chin, my eyes focusing in on Ash. "What do I need to do?"

"Take it." With a shaking hand, I took the piece of paper just as Ash lit a match and held it out. "Repeat after me... As burns this saint, so burns my soul. I enter alive and will have to get out dead."

"As burns this saint"—I gulped—"so burns my soul. I enter alive and will have to get out dead."

"Now burn," Ash said.

I held the paper to the flame and watched it turn into ash between my fingertips.

"*Sangue en, no fuori*," Ash said.

Blood in, no out.

Everyone repeated it at once, causing chills to run up and down my spine as Ash then put a hand on my shoulder and pulled me in, kissing my right cheek, and my left. "You chose this. You chose blood."

I lifted my head high. "There was never a choice, Ash. And if there was, I made it two years ago."

Tiny stopped in front of me, her smile so perfect and wide. The girl I'd always promised to rescue, now in love with a mafia prince.

"You did good," she whispered before kissing each cheek and then hugging me.

The bosses went next, most likely seeing the pride glistening in my eyes as I held my head high, taking on what should have been my birthright. What should have been my throne.

Sergio was last.

He was either going to kiss me or kill me.

I tensed when he stopped in front of me.

All I could hear was the buzzing in my ears as he turned to Tiny and said, "Are you free?"

A tear slid down her cheek as she whispered, "Yes."

"Then I won't kill him," Sergio said so matter-of-factly, I wanted to hurl as he turned his face back to mine. "Hurt her with your hands, I cut them off. Speak any ill of her with your tongue, and you'll never speak again. Betray my Family, and I'll make you blind so the last thing you see before I slit your throat is the very darkness you'll be damned to. Do you understand?"

"Yes, sir."

"Good." He leaned in and kissed both cheeks, then slapped me on the shoulder. "We'll talk later. Tonight..." He eyed Kartini. "I don't want to know what happens tonight, just keep her safe."

"Always have. Always will," I vowed.

"This...I know." His smile was small, but it was there.

I was still stunned into silence as the rest of the cousins and I walked back toward our bungalow.

Until, of course, Maksim interrupted. "I think you're the first De Lange to be welcomed in like...years."

"No pressure, though, really," King added.

"Yeah, I mean, it's not like he's going to die now..." Junior joked and then gave me a playful shove.

Kartini shoved Junior back.

Junior's eyebrows shot up. "The small one came out to play."

Kartini shoved him again. "I may be small but—"

"She killed a guy. I would tread lightly," Maksim grumbled.

Kartini gasped.

And then everyone paused.

He paled. "Shit. Sorry. I'm still slightly drunk."

King smacked him. "You were drinking without me?"

"Serena's fucking ruthless. Drank me under the table." He stumbled a bit.

Serena pulled at least a few hundred dollars out of her pocket. "Miss this, Maks?"

Maksim flipped her off.

Izzy just burst out laughing because she enjoyed Maksim's pain.

And then, out of nowhere, a body barreled toward me.

And my body flew into the pool.

I surfaced and then dove after Ash, who laughed like he'd just accomplished the impossible.

Taking me by surprise.

"You little shit, stop swimming away!" I grabbed his shirt.

And then, more splashes happened.

Clothes were yet again taken off and discarded in the moonlight as we all laughed and swam.

"You know, now that you're part of the Family, it's kind of weird that you guys were screwing in the cabana." King floated by me.

Everyone paused.

Maksim sighed and then shoved King to the bottom of the pool. "Should I drown him? Tell me the truth, Tiny?"

She just threw her head back and laughed. "No, let him breathe."

"Soooooo..." Izzy, Serena, and Annie swam headfirst toward Kartini. Her grin was huge as they all started whispering and pointing.

And then Ash and Junior were next to me.

"Those girls terrify me on a daily basis." Junior sighed. "But I love them."

"They're the best," Ash agreed.

Maksim floated by. "All but one."

"Last year, it was you sneaking into her house," I pointed out.

He sighed. "A lot of good my love did me."

I shared a look with Ash that said *let it go,* and King was already changing the subject yelling about drowning and how could we not care about his life as the next Capo?

I tuned him out.

Because I was going back to my bungalow with that woman. A smiling woman, no...not smiling, beaming.

Like she'd just been healed.

And I'd like to think I had a small part in that.

Chapter Twelve

Tank

It was like once I unlocked the sex goddess inside Kartini, she was insatiable...We stumbled back to our bedroom and slipped out of our wet clothes, falling into bed like it was normal.

She kissed me first.

And I wanted to tell her that I loved her first. Even when I wasn't supposed to, I did.

And now, now it felt like my heart might explode as I rolled her to her back and kissed down her neck, tasting the saltwater from the pool there.

"This was a good night." She wrapped her arms around me.

"The best."

Her eyebrows arched. "Is that a challenge?"

I was already so damn hard for her that my body ached. "Absolutely."

She sighed. "Tank, Tank, Tank, when will you ever learn? You can't win against me." She reached for my cock and squeezed.

"Fuck me." I threw my head back, wanting to roar. "Kind of feels like winning right now."

She slid her hand down, then back up. "We should probably slow down, though, so…"

With a menacing growl, I grabbed her hands and pinned them above her head. "That's a no."

"I kind of like being at your mercy." She shimmied, showing off her perfect, perky breasts and tanned skin.

"Question..."

"What?" Her smile was so open, so real.

"In the mafia, do we get to pick where we die?"

She burst out laughing. "Um, that would be a no since you never know where or why..."

"That's too bad." I leaned down and pressed my head between her breasts. "Because I pick here." I turned my mouth and kissed my way back up toward her neck and whispered, "And here." My kiss lingered at the corner of her mouth as I teased her entrance with my cock. "And maybe here, too."

She panted beneath me. "No arguments on my end, Tank. But fair warning, if you put in a request to die between my boobs, my dad's going to run you over with his Lambo."

We both fell into fits of laughter as I surged forward, causing the headboard to slam against the wall.

"Whoops." I cursed.

"We'll pay damages." Tiny groaned. "Just don't stop."

So, I didn't.

We screwed.

We made love.

We kissed.

We laughed.

And the next morning, when she was still lying there, looking well and truly loved, I dressed and made one last walk of my old life.

My badge and gun both burned holes against my body as I took the trails back up to the main lobby and bar.

I dialed the number.

I wasn't surprised to hear a sigh on the other end as Thompsons answered. "Any news?"

"It wasn't them," I lied.

Thompsons was quiet for a few minutes while my heart raced, wondering what he would say until he finally broke the silence. "So, you've chosen."

"Was there ever a question what side I would choose? Family or FBI?"

"And you're positive they had nothing to do with my agent's murder?"

"Positive," I lied again. It was easy to, knowing what had happened with Kartini. "But, sir, you need to know, he didn't back down that day. None of my team backed down when I asked them to leave it. So, either you gave the order to continue, or someone else did."

"The hell?" he roared. "Tank, it was your team. Your call to make, not mine."

"It was a shit idea in the first place," I reminded him. "They're Family. They're loyal. Creating war after they worked so hard to have peace, it does nothing to help us. It only makes us their enemy. You have to see that. The Petrov Family isn't weak like we thought, not under Valerian's rule. And you do not want to piss that son of a bitch off—trust me."

"They're too strong, Tank. May I remind you that the minute the Russians and Italians joined forces, they became a nightmare?"

"They've been quiet, and you know it. You're just afraid they're too strong. Powerful. You're afraid they're a fucking mafia monopoly, but hurting an innocent person just to get them to fight doesn't make you better, sir. It makes you worse than them."

"Anything else?" he snapped.

"Yeah." I paced. "I'm handing in my badge and gun to Giana once I find her."

"What the hell is Giana doing down there?" he roared. "Are you sure?"

My body went cold. "She said you sanctioned it. That you didn't trust me to get intel on my own."

"Tank, Giána was fired two days ago for insubordination."

"Fuck!" I roared into my phone. "I left her alone, I left her alone!"

I hung up the phone as he was talking and ran back down the pathway to my bungalow, hoping to God I wasn't too late.

Because Giana was clearly unhinged.

And if I knew her…

She was here to finish what she'd started.

Chapter Thirteen

Kartini

I woke up and stretched my sore body, throwing my arms over my head and wondering how the hell I'd put off confessing everything to Tank for so long. Oh, I was sure we'd argue like crazy despite the sex, but that's what would make our relationship so fun.

The arguing.

And the making up.

And I had a feeling we'd have a lot of making up to do in the future since both of us had serious issues with backing down.

I reached for my phone and saw a text from Serena.

Serena: *Hey, lover, going to the pool. When you pull that sore body out of Tank's arms, come join us. Then tell us all the details! Izzy wants to know if he almost broke you in half, how are you walking? Okay, okay just meet us asap!*

I laughed out loud. The text was only sent a few minutes ago. I fired one back.

Me: *Tell Izzy I might need crutches after last night, but it was worth it. And if he broke me in half, I'd ask him to do it again.*

Serena: *You WHORE!*

Me: *Izzy's just jealous because Chase cut down the tree Maksim used to sneak into the house and threatened bodily harm.*

Serena: *Um, he threatened decapitation but sure, same thing.*

Me: *Ughhhhhh, I'm tired. Okay, give me five minutes?*

Serena: *I'm ordering you booze, so you talk.*

Me: *That's to be expected.*

I threw the phone onto the bed and winced when I really did feel a bit of pain between my thighs. Geez, the guy had lost his mind last night.

Then again, I had, too.

I'd lost count after around six a.m.

And then I realized that I didn't need to count, did I?

Because what I had with him, it felt…real. Like forever.

Still grinning, I put on my black bikini then grabbed my Airpods, sunglasses, and keycard.

I was still smiling as I pushed open the suite doors and lifted my head, only to see a complete stranger sitting on my couch, a Glock 17 in her hand as she watched me with hatred dripping from every pore of her body.

I kept my head high. "You the maid?"

Her nostrils flared. "Do maids typically carry guns?"

"Good question." I crossed my arms and tried to memorize every detail of her face from her dark hair in a severe, tight bun, to her green eyes, to the way her pale skin seemed to glisten with sweat.

She was either nervous or unhinged.

Dressed in black leggings and a tight, matching t-shirt.

"You going to a funeral?" I joked.

She shook her head. "You really do have a mouth on you. Is that how you killed Jenner?"

I flinched. "Jenner?"

"FBI. My team member. Jenner."

Shit, shit, shit.

"I don't remember, there've been so many guys that…" I shrugged. "Is there a reason you're in my room? I mean, I get it, you're FBI, but have I done something wrong, agent…?" I waited.

"Giana," she said. "My name's Giana."

"Pretty name. Italian?"

"You killed them. You killed all of them! You killed my brother. My father." Her face went bright red. "And you killed Jenner, I know you did. And now, I'm going to kill you. That's why I'm here. Funny how the downfall of the De Lange line didn't break the Five Families but made them stronger. It's complete bullshit." She was almost talking to herself. "Do you hear me? Bullshit!"

I held up my hands. "I hear you. I do. I'm sorry about your brother and dad."

"No, you're not!" She jumped to her feet. "The mafia's never sorry. Chase Abandonato is a motherfucking senator! You think he's ever going to be tried for his sins? For assassinating an entire family line!"

I sighed. "I'm not justifying what he did, but you do realize what the De Lange Family is guilty of, right? Why they were pushed out of the fold? And even now, we still welcome them back in. But everything comes at a price."

"Death is death." She sneered. "And it doesn't bring them back. But I can get vengeance. Why else work for the law? Why not take it into my own hands?"

"Except..." came Tank's voice. When the hell had he snuck in? "You don't work for the FBI anymore, do you Giana?"

"Shut up!" She pointed the gun at him, then back at me. "You're dead to me. You chose THEM!"

"Yes." Tank nodded slowly. "Thompsons said you could have your old job back, Giana. You just need to put the gun down."

She faltered. "He wouldn't... He found out too much."

"Call him yourself." He jerked his head toward the table. "He just told me. Said I should turn my badge in to you."

He reached into his pocket and threw the badge at her, giving me enough time to kick the gun out of her hand while he tackled her to the floor.

I scrambled for the Glock, grabbed it, and turned it on her while Tank punched her in the face, knocking her out cold.

Shaking, I held the weapon out to him. "Well, that was a dramatic post-sex experience."

"Come here." He pulled me against his chest at about the same time my door burst open with my dad charging in, a gun in each hand. The rest of the bosses followed, and then they peered around us and laughed.

"She's out, all right." Dad picked up her arm and dropped it. "I'm assuming Tank's work?"

Tank held me tightly. "Actually, your daughter kicked the gun away. I got to take the punch."

"Next time, I get to punch," I grumbled. "Punching's more fun."

"Bloodthirsty little girl," Tank said under his breath.

"I'm not small," I argued.

All the men stared at me as if I had two heads.

"I'm delicate." I sniffed.

That got a laugh out of Tank.

"What happened? All I know is Tank was running toward your bungalow, so I assumed the worst…" Dad asked.

I filled them in on what happened, shocking the hell out of my dad and the rest of the bosses as they discussed a point of action for Giana. Tank said he'd talk to the local authorities and put her under arrest, and an agent would fly her back to the States for disciplinary action.

Which didn't sound fun.

By the time they were all done talking, and the proper authorities had taken Giana away—kicking and screaming, mind you —I was exhausted, starving, and really wanted a margarita.

Dad came over and kissed me on the forehead. "I'm leaving you in good hands, but let's try for no more attempted killing these next few months, all right?"

I nodded. "I'll try."

His expression was grim. "Maybe try a little harder. Your mother already threatened me last night after I told her what happened to you last year."

I laughed. "She use her favorite knife?"

"Carries that thing everywhere, you know that."

I laughed.

He paused for a second, his eyes searching mine. "I love you, Tiny. I will always love you more than my life, more than my next breath— blood staining your hands or not. You're mine."

A tear slid down my cheek before I could stop it as I rushed into his arms, slamming my face against his chest. Dad always smelled so good, he was so strong, so perfect.

My hero.

"I'm s-sorry."

"Don't be," he whispered. "Just promise you won't make it easy for Tank, all right?"

"I'll give him hell." I sniffled.

Dad barked out a laugh. "I believe it. Now, go relax…"

His face went a bit red.

"Dad, is *relax* a code word for sex?"

"Oh, God." Dad backed up slowly.

"Daddy, where do babies come from?" I teased as he started

walking away from me. "But, Daddy, I need to know!"

"She's your problem now, Tank," Dad called after him. "Good luck!"

"You're abandoning me?" Tank yelled.

The door shut.

"You're impossible." Tank rested his chin on my head. "You should go easy on him, he's getting old…"

"No, you're old."

"This again?"

"The truth? Yes, Tank."

"How about"—he spun me around in his arms—"we go hang out with everyone at the pool? They have nachos, margaritas…"

"Mmmmmm." I wrapped my arms around him. "Sounds great. But first…" I took his shorts down with me as I went to my knees. "I think it's only right that I thank my hero for coming after me."

"Gonna be coming before you if you keep looking at me like that," he teased.

I gripped him in my hand. "Yeah, you will."

"Damn, your mouth…" He dug his hands into my hair. "I don't deserve you."

"Nope." I licked his tip.

He shuddered. "God, you're annoying."

"I bite."

"But I love you anyway…" His body shuddered.

I looked up. "You love me?"

Tank frowned. "I loved you the minute you finally started talking to me last year and tripped me then said, 'Oh, hey.'"

I laughed. "That was a good day."

"I loved you when you told me to go die too, but it was more of an *I love her, but I hate her when she says that with her mouth—while her eyes drink me in.*"

"I was afraid."

"Let your fear go…." His eyes were heavy. "You're mine now."

"Yes." I returned my attention to his very perfect body. "You are."

Chapter Fourteen

Tank

"Some vacation." I grinned while Junior and Serena exchanged vows out in front of the ocean. It was perfect.

Scary, but perfect.

And only scary because somehow Serena had convinced every single boss/uncle sitting up front to wear matching white linen shirts.

Meaning, all I saw were angry tattoos swirling around their crossed arms, and the guns strapped to their chests below the clothing.

They were their own army.

And the pictures? Well, they would definitely show the weapons. Poor caterers kept tripping in the sand as they set up the reception out closer to the water.

It would be hilarious to watch if I didn't understand that fear very well. My first time meeting them, I'd nearly shit myself.

Now, it was a bit easier.

Because one of their princesses was entrusted to me.

"Yeah." Kartini clung to my arm as we watched them make their promises. "It started at a wedding, and the drama ends at the wedding.'

"The drama." I beamed down at her in her gorgeous, tan peasant dress and blue heels that matched her eyes. "But not us."

"Never us." She licked her lips and then frowned behind me. "Plus, I have a birthday to celebrate later this week."

"Birthday sex," Maksim slurred to himself as he slumped in his chair. King kept kicking him. I'd seen that look on Maksim's face before.

He was pissed.

Which meant, he must have fought with Izzy again.

"You okay?" I elbowed him. "Maksim?"

"No." His eyes were hollow, lost. "No, I'm not."

"Do you want to talk about it?"

"Ha…" He kicked some sand with his shoe. "No, Tank. I don't want to talk. I want to drink. And I want to fuck. And then I want to do some math."

"Ummm, okay."

"Likes his math, turns him on," King said from the other side of him. "Just…relax a bit, bro, then we'll get you some coffee."

King shot me a worried glance.

I turned back to Tiny. "What's going on with him?"

Her expression shuddered. "Not my story to tell."

"Ah, one of those."

"Yeah." She gulped. "But I don't see a happy ending with his. I don't see an ending at all if he keeps at it."

"We're family." I reached for her hand. "We'll be there for him, the way he was there for you."

She smiled up at me. "How did I get so lucky to find such a mature old man with such a large dick to be my boyfriend?"

Annie choked and started coughing behind us while Ash leaned forward and patted me on the back. "Well done, sir."

"Thank you." I winked at him while Annie covered her red face with her hands, and Kartini just shrugged as if to say, *"Well, it is."*

I loved that woman.

The ceremony was short.

The vows were beautiful.

And the next thing I knew, I was eating lobster next to Sergio and wondering if he prayed for me to choke on my next bite as he seemed to purposefully crack the shell open with too much vigor.

"So…" I started.

"No small talk." He pointed a claw at me. "You're moving your shit into the pool house." He waved the claw around. "I'm not stupid. I know she'll sneak in, but I figure the more distance I put between you two, the better."

"Wait. I can still live with you?" I was stunned.

He frowned. "Why would I kick you out?"

"Well, that's really nice of—"

"It's so much easier to spy on you under my roof."

I gulped. "Awesome."

"Come on!" Kartini grabbed my hand. "It's time to dance!"

She pulled me to my feet before I could say anything else to Sergio, and then I forgot all about his grumpy look when Tiny danced around me.

When I joined my friends on the dance floor.

Beneath the stars.

My Family.

Finally, I'd come home.

Epilogue

Kartini

Six months later

Tank: *Gonna be home in a few, had one more errand to run.*
    Me: *Sounds good!*

I threw my phone onto my bed and watched my best friend pace a hole in the floor. "I should just call him, right?"

I groaned into my hands. "Look, Izzy, you just need to fix all of this. It's causing stress between everyone."

Her eyes filled with tears. "But Dad—"

"He let Serena and Junior be together," I pointed out.

She nearly snarled. "You don't even know. They nearly died. This is different, trust me. If you had seen his face..."

"He's understanding."

"Ha. My dad? Mine? Chase Abandonato?"

I winced. "He loves you."

"Too much. It's possible to love someone so much that you smother them to death. He's killing me!"

Someone knocked on my bedroom door.

"It's open," I called.

Mom poked her head in. "Iz, your dad's downstairs, he's ready to take you home for dinner."

She clenched her teeth. "Fine."

"We're in a good mood." She grinned.

Izzy looked ready to scream as she stomped by her and out the door.

"Oh, and Tiny? Tank wanted me to give you this." She tossed a burner phone to me.

"Huh?"

She just smiled.

It rang seconds later, when my mom was gone.

I answered it on the third ring. "Hello?"

"This is your mission if you choose to accept it." Tank's voice came on the line. "Look out the window and tell me yes or no."

"What?" I laughed. "Are you drunk?"

"Just do it..." His voice was rough, dark. Mine.

"Fine…" I crawled off my bed and went over to the window, and gasped as I saw all of my friends and cousins standing outside.

They'd recreated Mexico in my backyard.

And in the very front was Tank, in a tux.

I would truly never recover from seeing that large man fit into a tux, his eyes bright.

He held the phone against his ear. "So, yes or no?"

"What are you asking?"

I nearly dropped the cell when he went down on one knee. "I was going to do this so many different ways, but I realized if I did it right in front of you, I'd sob like a baby, you'd call me out on it, and then I wouldn't get through it."

My eyes filled with tears. "Kartini Abandonato, I love you with my entire heart and soul. With my life. Will you please do me the honor of becoming my wife?"

I threw the phone onto my bed and sprinted.

I sprinted down the stairs and out the door, and in typical *me* fashion, I tackled that wonderful man onto the grass and kissed him.

When he came up for air, he asked, "Was that a yes?"

"Shut up!" I shoved him a bit then kissed him again. "And, yes, that's a hell yes."

"Ah, little girl always has to make a scene."

"I love you."

"I love you, too." His eyes filled with tears then.

He was on the Abandonato payroll and had been working a lot lately. I didn't ask him about the blood on his hands or how he seemed to mature even more as the bosses asked him to move into the captain position under Nixon's leadership.

I assumed he'd been stressed.

Not that he was planning this and nervous.

"Our lives won't be normal," I said once I stood and took his hand.

"Good." He towered over me and pulled me into his arms. "I don't want normal. I want this crazy girl with blue in her hair, who likes to defy authority."

I lifted my chin. "A princess bows to no one."

"True."

"Except her king." She winked and then did a little curtsy. "Your Majesty."

With a growl, he pulled me into his arms again. "I'm so glad you're mine."

"Yours. Forever."

Everyone cheered around us.

And when the music started, and I danced on Tank's feet like I used to with my dad, I knew. I'd been forced to grow up, but I'd needed it.

From one true love to another.

From one mafia king to the next.

And when Dad looked away and swiped at his cheek just briefly...

I smiled.

Because I would always be his, too.

And he knew it.

* * * *

Also from 1001 Dark Nights and Rachel Van Dyken, discover Provoke, Abandon, All Stars Fall, and Envy.

Sign up for the 1001 Dark Nights Newsletter
and be entered to win a Tiffany Key necklace.

There's a contest every month!

Go to www.1001DarkNights.com to subscribe.

As a bonus, all subscribers can download
FIVE FREE exclusive books!

Discover 1001 Dark Nights Collection Eight

DRAGON REVEALED by Donna Grant
A Dragon Kings Novella

CAPTURED IN INK by Carrie Ann Ryan
A Montgomery Ink: Boulder Novella

SECURING JANE by Susan Stoker
A SEAL of Protection: Legacy Series Novella

WILD WIND by Kristen Ashley
A Chaos Novella

DARE TO TEASE by Carly Phillips
A Dare Nation Novella

VAMPIRE by Rebecca Zanetti
A Dark Protectors/Rebels Novella

MAFIA KING by Rachel Van Dyken
A Mafia Royals Novella

THE GRAVEDIGGER'S SON by Darynda Jones
A Charley Davidson Novella

FINALE by Skye Warren
A North Security Novella

MEMORIES OF YOU by J. Kenner
A Stark Securities Novella

SLAYED BY DARKNESS by Alexandra Ivy
A Guardians of Eternity Novella

TREASURED by Lexi Blake
A Masters and Mercenaries Novella

THE DAREDEVIL by Dylan Allen
A Rivers Wilde Novella

BOND OF DESTINY by Larissa Ione
A Demonica Novella

THE CLOSE-UP by Kennedy Ryan
A Hollywood Renaissance Novella

MORE THAN POSSESS YOU by Shayla Black
A More Than Words Novella

HAUNTED HOUSE by Heather Graham
A Krewe of Hunters Novella

MAN FOR ME by Laurelin Paige
A Man In Charge Novella

THE RHYTHM METHOD by Kylie Scott
A Stage Dive Novella

JONAH BENNETT by Tijan
A Bennett Mafia Novella

CHANGE WITH ME by Kristen Proby
A With Me In Seattle Novella

THE DARKEST DESTINY by Gena Showalter
A Lords of the Underworld Novella

Also from Blue Box Press

THE LAST TIARA by M.J. Rose

THE CROWN OF GILDED BONES by Jennifer L. Armentrout
A Blood and Ash Novel

THE MISSING SISTER by Lucinda Riley

Discover More Rachel Van Dyken

Provoke: A Seaside Pictures Novella
By Rachel Van Dyken

The music industry called me a savant at age sixteen when I uploaded my first video and gained instant fame. And then Drew Amherst of Adrenaline became my mentor, and my career took off.

Everything was great.

Until tragedy struck, and I wondered if I'd ever be able to perform again. I fought back, but all it took was a falling light to bring it all back to the fore. So, I walked away. Because I knew it wasn't just stage fright. It was so much more.

The only problem?

Drew and the guys are counting on me. If I can't combat the crippling anxiety threatening to kill me, I might lose more than I ever dreamed of.

Enter Piper Rayne, life coach, with her bullshit about empowerment, rainbows, and butterflies. She smiles all the damn time, and I'm ninety-nine percent sure there's not a problem she can't solve.

Until me.

She was given twenty-one days to fix me. To make me see what's important. What's real. The problem is, all I can see now is her. The sexy woman who pushes me. Provokes me.

Only time will tell if she's able to do her job—and I can make her mine.

* * * *

Abandon: A Seaside Pictures Novella
By Rachel Van Dyken

It's not every day you're slapped on stage by two different women you've been dating for the last year.

I know what you're thinking. What sort of ballsy woman gets on stage and slaps a rockstar? Does nobody have self-control anymore? It may have been the talk of the Grammys.

Oh, yeah, forgot to mention that. I, Ty Cuban, was taken down by two psychotic women in front of the entire world. Lucky for us the audience thought it was part of the breakup song my band and I had just finished performing. I was thirty-three, hardly ready to settle down.

Except now it's getting forced on me. Seaside, Oregon. My bandmates were more than happy to settle down, dig their roots into the sand, and start popping out kids. Meanwhile I was still enjoying life.

Until now. Until my forced hiatus teaching freaking guitar lessons at the local studio for the next two months. Part of my punishment, do something for the community while I think deep thoughts about all my life choices.

Sixty days of hell.

It doesn't help that the other volunteer is a past flame that literally looks at me as if I've sold my soul to the devil. She has the voice of an angel and looks to kill—I would know, because she looks ready to kill me every second of every day. I broke her heart when we were on tour together a decade ago.

I'm ready to put the past behind us. She's ready to run me over with her car then stand on top of it and strum her guitar with glee.

Sixty days. I can do anything for sixty days. Including making the sexy Von Abigail fall for me all over again. This time for good.

Damn, maybe there's something in the water.

* * * *

All Stars Fall: A Seaside Pictures/Big Sky Novella
By Rachel Van Dyken

She *left*.
Two words I can't really get out of my head.
She left *us*.
Three more words that make it that much worse.
Three being another word I can't seem to wrap my mind around.
Three kids under the age of six, and she left because she missed it. Because her dream had never been to have a family, no, her dream had been to marry a rockstar and live the high life.

Moving my recording studio to Seaside Oregon seems like the best idea in the world right now especially since Seaside Oregon has turned into the place for celebrities to stay and raise families in between touring and producing. It would be lucrative to make the move, but I'm doing it for my kids because they need normal, they deserve normal. And me?

Well, I just need a break and help, that too. I need a sitter and fast. Someone who won't flip me off when I ask them to sign an Iron Clad NDA, someone who won't sell our pictures to the press, and most of all? Someone who looks absolutely nothing like my ex-wife.

He's tall.

That was my first instinct when I saw the notorious Trevor Wood, drummer for the rock band Adrenaline, in the local coffee shop. He ordered a tall black coffee which made me smirk, and five minutes later I somehow agreed to interview for a nanny position. I couldn't help it; the smaller one had gum stuck in her hair while the eldest was standing on his feet and asking where babies came from. He looked so pathetic, so damn sexy and pathetic that rather than be star-struck, I took pity. I knew though; I knew the minute I signed that NDA, the minute our fingers brushed and my body became insanely aware of how close he was—I was in dangerous territory, I just didn't know how dangerous until it was too late. Until I fell for the star and realized that no matter how high they are in the sky—they're still human and fall just as hard.

* * * *

Envy: An Eagle Elite Novella
By Rachel Van Dyken

Every family has rules, the mafia just has more....
Do not speak to the bosses unless spoken to.
Do not make eye contact unless you want to die.
And above all else, do not fall in love.
Renee Cassani's future is set.
Her betrothal is set.
Her life, after nannying for the five families for the summer, is set.
Somebody should have told Vic Colezan that.
He's a man who doesn't take no for an answer.
And he only wants one thing.
Her.
Somebody should have told Renee that her bodyguard needed as much discipline as the kids she was nannying.
Good thing Vic has a firm hand.

Destructive King: A Mafia Bully Romance
Mafia Royals Book 3
By Rachel Van Dyken

A mafia romance about love and loss by Rachel Van Dyken, the number one *New York Times* bestselling author of the Eagle Elite series.

...When you awaken in the morning's hush
I am the swift uplifting rush
Of quiet birds in circled flight.
I am the soft stars that shine at night.
Do not stand at my grave and cry;
I am not there. I did not die.
— Mary Elizabeth Fyre

"I'm sorry for your loss." I would rather be tortured for an eternity than hear those damn words from one more person, as if Claire, my dead fiancé, was a cell phone or car keys.

How about, I'm sorry your life is over.

I'm sorry you want to die too.

I'm sorry you see her in your dreams and wake up only to relive the nightmare.

I'm supposed to be the strongest of them all. Ash Abandonato, ruler, assassin, made man, brother, friend—instead, I hurt everyone I touch in hopes that they'll feel even a sliver of the pain that bears down on my shoulders.

I didn't lose.

It was taken from me.

And it's all her fault, Annie Smith.

I daydream about her death.

And then I close my eyes, and I see her soft smile. I feel her touch, her kiss—it was a mistake what we did that night, but I can't take it back, and now she's under my father's protection—my protection.

My worst enemy.

The woman I'm the most attracted to.

I can't decide if I want to strangle her or kiss her, and now that she's stuck in my life, my only goal is to make her feel the same loss I do and destroy her in the process.

I'll trick her with my touch.

Seduce her with my kiss.

And in the end, when my enemy is at her most vulnerable—I'll bring down an entire Empire and continue my reign as King.

Bow down, I'll say as I bring the Five Families to their knees.

Blood in.

Never out.

Damned.

* * * *

A light flickered from the bathroom.

I sighed in relief, then went over and knocked, the door creaked open, and there he was, sitting in the bathtub completely naked.

It was impossible not to notice his perfect physique; even drunk out of his mind, he was beautiful—like a fallen angel that forgot his place was in Heaven—not his own personal hell.

"You know…" He held out a giant knife and thumbed the blade, studying the point as a trickle of blood trailed down his thumb. "Most people do it wrong…"

I froze. "You're drunk, Ash. Let's just get you some clothes—"

"Fucking idiots." His pupils were pinpoints as he looked at me over the blade of the knife. "They cut against the vein forgetting that you're supposed to cut with it. But there's other ways, Claire—other ways to join you…"

He was out of his mind. My chest heaved with panic as I weighed my options. He was an expert at killing things, even drunk. I was a college nerd on scholarship who had zero hand-to-hand combat skills.

Let alone against a proven killer.

"Three seconds," he rasped as he lowered the knife to the inside of his thigh. "Three seconds, and I'll see you, sweetheart. Three seconds and you'll be real again, three seconds, and we'll be a family." Tears streamed down his face. "That's all, Claire. That's all it would take."

The knife was so dangerously close to his femoral artery that I had no time to call Chase or the ambulance.

No time but to figure out a way to save his life.

No other way.

"Don't," I whispered. "Ash, please…don't."

"I have to." He sobbed. "I have to!"

"Please!" I choked on my tears. "Please don't, Ash, please! Just stay, stay with me, right here, right now—hand me the knife."

"Three seconds, Claire."

"Ash, Claire would want you to live."

"I killed you..." He grabbed the blade with his other hand and squeezed as blood spurted all over the bathtub. "This may as well be your blood. You were my soul, and I spilled it, I spilled it all. I didn't see, I didn't—" The knife slipped out of his bloody hand.

I lunged for it and barely grabbed it in time before he did; he was thankfully too slow.

I threw the knife away from us; it clattered against the bathroom floor as I tripped against his legs as they dangled out of the tub.

With a grunt, I fell on top of him.

He held me there.

Bleeding on me.

Sobbing.

His arms came around me. "You're gone, you're gone!"

I squeezed my eyes shut as he held me close, and then he was kissing the back of my neck.

"It's Annie..." I moved away from him. "I'm not Claire—"

"Claire..." He moaned. "Please..."

"Ash," I said it more firmly that time. "It's Annie."

I finally broke free from him, but he was fast; he grabbed me again, this time shoving up from the bathtub and reaching for me, jerking me against his chest as he pressed a hungry kiss to my mouth.

Every time I tried to pull away, he pulled me back.

And then he was turning the shower on.

My sweatshirt was coming off.

Escape was futile.

"Claire—"

"Ash." My heart cracked in half.

He stole it then.

He stomped on it.

He wrecked it like he wrecked everything.

And I let him because I was too afraid he'd kill himself.

Too afraid that he'd snap.

I'd always been too afraid.

And half in love with a man who loved a ghost and would do

anything to follow her into Heaven.

"Until the sky falls…" he whispered as he kissed me again and again, so I said the only thing I could say back.

The only thing I'd ever heard Claire repeat over and over again.

"Even," I whispered, "Until the sky falls, Ash."

"You're here…" He smiled for the first time. "Finally…finally…"

A tear slid down my cheek and joined the blood, and whatever was left of my broken heart as I swore to take this to my grave.

Right along with any feelings I'd ever had for Ash Abandonato.

He may as well be dead.

I may as well have let him do the digging.

"Goodbye, Ash," I whispered under my breath.

This time I kissed him.

This time I pulled him.

This time I gave him what he'd been wanting since yelling into the dark night sky—Claire.

I gave him Claire.

About Rachel Van Dyken

Rachel Van Dyken is the #1 New York Times, Wall Street Journal, and USA Today bestselling author of over 90 books ranging from contemporary romance to paranormal. With over four million copies sold, she's been featured in Forbes, US Weekly, and USA Today. Her books have been translated in more than 15 countries. She was one of the first romance authors to have a Kindle in Motion book through Amazon publishing and continues to strive to be on the cutting edge of the reader experience. She keeps her home in the Pacific Northwest with her husband, adorable sons, naked cat, and lazy dog.

You can connect with her on Facebook:
www.facebook.com/rachelvandyken
or join her fan group Rachel's New Rockin Readers:
https://www.facebook.com/groups/RRRFanClub.

For more information, visit her website at
http://rachelvandykenauthor.com.

Discover 1001 Dark Nights

THE ONLY ONE by Lauren Blakely ~ SWEET SURRENDER by Liliana Hart

COLLECTION FOUR
ROCK CHICK REAWAKENING by Kristen Ashley ~ ADORING INK by Carrie Ann Ryan ~ SWEET RIVALRY by K. Bromberg ~ SHADE'S LADY by Joanna Wylde ~ RAZR by Larissa Ione ~ ARRANGED by Lexi Blake ~ TANGLED by Rebecca Zanetti ~ HOLD ME by J. Kenner ~ SOMEHOW, SOME WAY by Jennifer Probst ~ TOO CLOSE TO CALL by Tessa Bailey ~ HUNTED by Elisabeth Naughton ~ EYES ON YOU by Laura Kaye ~ BLADE by Alexandra Ivy/Laura Wright ~ DRAGON BURN by Donna Grant ~ TRIPPED OUT by Lorelei James ~ STUD FINDER by Lauren Blakely ~ MIDNIGHT UNLEASHED by Lara Adrian ~ HALLOW BE THE HAUNT by Heather Graham ~ DIRTY FILTHY FIX by Laurelin Paige ~ THE BED MATE by Kendall Ryan ~ NIGHT GAMES by CD Reiss ~ NO RESERVATIONS by Kristen Proby ~ DAWN OF SURRENDER by Liliana Hart

COLLECTION FIVE
BLAZE ERUPTING by Rebecca Zanetti ~ ROUGH RIDE by Kristen Ashley ~ HAWKYN by Larissa Ione ~ RIDE DIRTY by Laura Kaye ~ ROME'S CHANCE by Joanna Wylde ~ THE MARRIAGE ARRANGEMENT by Jennifer Probst ~ SURRENDER by Elisabeth Naughton ~ INKED NIGHTS by Carrie Ann Ryan ~ ENVY by Rachel Van Dyken ~ PROTECTED by Lexi Blake ~ THE PRINCE by Jennifer L. Armentrout ~ PLEASE ME by J. Kenner ~ WOUND TIGHT by Lorelei James ~ STRONG by Kylie Scott ~ DRAGON NIGHT by Donna Grant ~ TEMPTING BROOKE by Kristen Proby ~ HAUNTED BE THE HOLIDAYS by Heather Graham ~ CONTROL by K. Bromberg ~ HUNKY HEARTBREAKER by Kendall Ryan ~ THE DARKEST CAPTIVE by Gena Showalter

COLLECTION SIX
DRAGON CLAIMED by Donna Grant ~ ASHES TO INK by Carrie Ann Ryan ~ ENSNARED by Elisabeth Naughton ~ EVERMORE by Corinne Michaels ~ VENGEANCE by Rebecca Zanetti ~ ELI'S TRIUMPH by Joanna Wylde ~ CIPHER by Larissa Ione ~ RESCUING MACIE by Susan Stoker ~ ENCHANTED by Lexi Blake

~ TAKE THE BRIDE by Carly Phillips ~ INDULGE ME by J. Kenner ~ THE KING by Jennifer L. Armentrout ~ QUIET MAN by Kristen Ashley ~ ABANDON by Rachel Van Dyken ~ THE OPEN DOOR by Laurelin Paige~ CLOSER by Kylie Scott ~ SOMETHING JUST LIKE THIS by Jennifer Probst ~ BLOOD NIGHT by Heather Graham ~ TWIST OF FATE by Jill Shalvis ~ MORE THAN PLEASURE YOU by Shayla Black ~ WONDER WITH ME by Kristen Proby ~ THE DARKEST ASSASSIN by Gena Showalter

COLLECTION SEVEN

THE BISHOP by Skye Warren ~ TAKEN WITH YOU by Carrie Ann Ryan ~ DRAGON LOST by Donna Grant ~ SEXY LOVE by Carly Phillips ~ PROVOKE by Rachel Van Dyken ~ RAFE by Sawyer Bennett ~ THE NAUGHTY PRINCESS by Claire Contreras ~ THE GRAVEYARD SHIFT by Darynda Jones ~ CHARMED by Lexi Blake ~ SACRIFICE OF DARKNESS by Alexandra Ivy ~ THE QUEEN by Jen Armentrout ~ BEGIN AGAIN by Jennifer Probst ~ VIXEN by Rebecca Zanetti ~ SLASH by Laurelin Paige ~ THE DEAD HEAT OF SUMMER by Heather Graham ~ WILD FIRE by Kristen Ashley ~ MORE THAN PROTECT YOU by Shayla Black ~ LOVE SONG by Kylie Scott ~ CHERISH ME by J. Kenner ~ SHINE WITH ME by Kristen Proby

Discover Blue Box Press

TAME ME by J. Kenner ~ TEMPT ME by J. Kenner ~ DAMIEN by J. Kenner ~ TEASE ME by J. Kenner ~ REAPER by Larissa Ione ~ THE SURRENDER GATE by Christopher Rice ~ SERVICING THE TARGET by Cherise Sinclair ~ THE LAKE OF LEARNING by Steve Berry and MJ Rose ~ THE MUSEUM OF MYSTERIES by Steve Berry and MJ Rose ~ TEASE ME by J. Kenner ~ FROM BLOOD AND ASH by Jennifer L. Armentrout ~ QUEEN MOVE by Kennedy Ryan ~ THE HOUSE OF LONG AGO by Steve Berry and MJ Rose ~ THE BUTTERFLY ROOM by Lucinda Riley ~ A KINGDOM OF FLESH AND FIRE by Jennifer L. Armentrout

On behalf of 1001 Dark Nights,

Liz Berry, M.J. Rose, and Jillian Stein would like to thank ~

Steve Berry
Doug Scofield
Benjamin Stein
Kim Guidroz
Social Butterfly PR
Ashley Wells
Asha Hossain
Chris Graham
Chelle Olson
Kasi Alexander
Jessica Johns
Dylan Stockton
Richard Blake
and Simon Lipskar